OFF THE BEATEN HEART

ROWAN PIERCE

Copyright © [2024] by [Rowan Pierce]

All rights reserved.

No portion of this book may be reproduced in any form without written permission from the publisher or author, except as permitted by U.S. copyright law.

Contents

1. Chapter One- The Meeting — 1
2. Chapter Two- The Conflict — 6
3. Chapter Three- Creative Synergy — 11
4. Chapter Four- Push and Pull — 17
5. Chapter Five- Fractured Perspective — 23
6. Chapter Six- Confessions — 28
7. Chapter Seven- Friend's Visit — 34
8. Chapter Eight- A Momentary High — 39
9. Chapter Nine- Confrontation — 45
10. Chapter Ten- The Silent Rift — 50
11. Chapter Eleven-The Collapse — 56
12. Chapter Twelve- Self Reflection — 61
13. Chapter Thirteen- Reconnection — 66
14. Chapter Fourteen- The Final Verse — 72

15.	Chapter Fifteen- The Choice	78
16.	Concluding Thoughts	83
17.	Straight from the Heart	87

CHAPTER ONE - THE MEETING

Staring at the blank document on his laptop screen, Ethan Carter sat at his desk. The blinking cursor, which had been pulsing in the same rhythmic manner for the past three days, appeared to be mocking him. Every blink seemed to be a reminder of his mounting annoyance, a quiet test to see if he had anything else to say. With a heavy sigh, he combed through his messy hair. Although his most recent book had been a minor success and received positive reviews from fans and critics, it hadn't moved him as much as his previous efforts had. It had no residual emotion, no magic. Like so much else in today's world, it was just a product.

Ethan had always found that writing allowed him to explore feelings, experiences, and the human condition on a deeper level. Now, however, he felt disconnected from his words in the never-ending chaos of a digital society full of transient connections and rapid pleasure. Once significant, stories seemed as fleeting as social media updates, absorbed and then forgotten within hours. Why should we produce something genuine and profound if it would disappear in the chaos?

The sound of his chair scraping the wood floor was a sharp break in the stillness of the room, and his irritation increased as he pushed it back. Even the normal vitality of the city of New York, which hummed outside, seemed muffled and distant. In his creative emptiness, the sounds of the streets were reduced to mere background static. He grabbed his coat and keys and whispered to himself, "I have to leave."

Before Ethan realized it, he was heading north, the expansive city behind him giving way to the undulating hills and serene landscape of upstate New York. He had no intention of leaving the city, yet he felt compelled to do so. He remembered, somewhere in his memory, a small, creative community tucked away in the hills—a place he had been to on one of his previous book tours years ago. The town was peaceful, relaxed, and teeming with artists who took comfort in the leisurely pace of life. Perhaps—just possibly—that was what he needed to rekindle the long-lost spark.

Ethan drove for several hours before reaching the town. It appeared nearly as he had remembered it, with streets lined with trees, quaint cafes, and a calm that contrasted sharply with the city's hustle and bustle. After parking, he stretched and inhaled deeply of the cool fall air. The location had a soothing quality. It seemed completely different from everything he had been thinking about lately. He dropped his suitcase in the corner of the charming cottage-style room and checked into a modest bed and breakfast. The aroma of lavender filled the room, and local artwork decorated the walls. He felt a strange sense of comfort here, as if this journey would allow him to let go of the words that had been stifling inside him. Ethan chose to tour the town after unpacking. He strolled along the cobblestone streets, pausing to take in the handcrafted goods on show in the storefront windows and the colorful murals painted on the walls of historic structures. This town's seeming resistance to the fast-paced modern world appealed to him. Instead of following trends, living in the moment and creating something meaningful was more important. He noticed a tiny art gallery tucked away between two coffee shops as he passed a row of eateries. From the outside, the gallery appeared modest, yet there was a pull that caused him to pause. He pushed the door open out of curiosity and entered.

The color immediately drew his attention. Abstract artwork that pulsed with emotion and energy adorned the walls. Vibrant bursts of yellow, blue, and red appeared to pop off the canvas, whirling in ways that were defying form and organization. This type of artwork evoked emotions before you could fully understand them. A voice emerged from his reverie, asking, "You like it?" Ethan turned to see a woman standing a few steps away, smiling playfully at him while crossing her arms. She appeared to be in her early thirties, with her wavy, wild hair twisted into a loose knot at the top of her head. The paint smears on her leggings and the green smudge on her cheek suggested that she had just emerged from one of her own paintings. There was a naughty intensity in her eyes that instantly piqued Ethan's interest. He looked back at the painting in front of him and honestly said, "I'm still figuring that out." "It's... different." A lot of movement is present.

The woman stepped closer and stated, "That's exactly what I was going for." " You shouldn't confine art to your thoughts. It should strike you and give you a slight jolt. Ethan nodded and grinned. "Are you the artist?" She held out her hand and said, "I feel guilty." Olivia Brooks. Good to meet you. He shook her hand and said "Ethan Carter." In contrast to his normal chilly reserve, he could feel the warmth of the energy in her grasp. "Ethan Carter." Olivia studied him, tilting her head. "The author, correct? I've already read one of your books. You've mastered the mood of the melancholy artist. Ethan laughed in surprise at her candor. "That clear?" She smirked and said,

"Not at all." But for ten minutes, you've been staring at that painting like a puzzle. We artists spend too much time in our imaginations. Her remarks resonated. Ethan realized he had done that overall, not just with the painting.

He was trying to comprehend everything instead of letting things unfold organically. He had been preoccupied with his next move, his next tale, and his next success for a long time, which had prevented him from being present in the moment. "How about you?" he asked, pointing to the paint-splattered clothing. "Do you just let the chaos happen every time?" Olivia smiled. I only know how to live that way. Life is too brief to dwell on it too much. They continued their chat, which flowed naturally between them. Ethan found Olivia's easygoing demeanor both fascinating and confusing. In contrast to him, she was spontaneous, unstructured, and completely unconcerned with the need for control. That same spirit was evident in her paintings, which were vibrant and wild with every brushstroke. They talked about increasingly intimate subjects as the evening went darker. Olivia's relationship philosophy surprised Ethan. "It's not that I don't think relationships are important," she clarified, her tone becoming softer. "I simply believe that they are under too much pressure. Everyone wants to give everything a definition, a label, and an everlasting status.

However, nothing in life is everlasting. Instead of attempting to manage our relationships, why not simply enjoy them?

Intrigued but unsure, Ethan listened. He has always supported the notion of dedication and creating a long-lasting relationship with another individual. Olivia's strategy appeared careless, almost innocent. Nevertheless, there was a beauty in her perspective—one that was free from the worries that often weighed him down. Later that evening, they said their goodbyes, but not before Olivia invited Ethan to attend one of her painting classes the next day. She smiled teasingly and said, "Come by my studio."

" Who knows? Perhaps a little mayhem is exactly what you need to get past your writer's block. Ethan kept thinking about Olivia as he made his way back to his bed and breakfast. For the first time in what seemed like an eternity, he felt a glimmer of excitement because she was unlike anyone he had ever met. Perhaps this location and this woman were just what he needed to reconnect with the words that had eluded him for so long.

Ethan felt the faintest spark of inspiration flicker in the back of his mind as he gazed up at the clear night sky. Even if it wasn't much, it was something. And that was sufficient for now.

Chapter Two - The Conflict

Ethan wasn't certain if he wanted to wake up from the dreamlike state that followed his encounter with Olivia. They drifted through the small town like a couple of free-spirited artists, going from gallery to gallery and café to café, spending almost every waking moment together. Every day was an adventure, with impromptu chats and detours that left Ethan feeling both excited and uneasy. He had never seen anything like Olivia's vitality, yet it came with a wildness that made him uneasy.

They strolled down the cobblestone streets, discussing everything from their divergent perspectives on life to art and creativity. There was no denying Olivia's intensity. She painted as carelessly as she had spent her life, and every brushstroke reflected her conviction that nothing needed to be defined or endured.

The burden of their disagreements started to weigh heavily on Ethan during one of their walks by the river. The river's soft sound served as a calming background for their chat, while the late afternoon sun gave the water a golden tint. With a little canvas resting on her knees and her brush moving in confident, swift strokes, Olivia sat

OFF THE BEATEN HEART

cross-legged on the grassy bank. Ethan, who had been unable to write down ideas for weeks prior to meeting her, was sitting next to her with his notebook. Olivia continued painting without raising her gaze. "You know," she added, "people spend so much time chasing forever." However, eternity is a myth, isn't it? Eventually, everything comes to an end.

Ethan pondered what she had said for a moment, his pen lingering over the paper. He answered slowly, "I'm not sure if I agree with that." "Some things endure. For example, love. Shouldn't genuine love last?

Olivia's brush continued to bounce across the canvas while her lips formed a gentle smile. "Ethan, the beauty of love lies in its fleeting nature." For anything to be genuine or significant, it doesn't have to endure forever. The relationships that fade the fastest are sometimes the ones that burn the brightest. This is the foundation of their strength.

Ethan felt something when she spoke, but he wasn't sure if it was curiosity or unease. He had always clung to the idea of enduring love and forming a bond with someone that would withstand the passage of time. His parents' lengthy marriage, a partnership that endured life's highs and lows for thirty years, demonstrated this. Even though his personal relationships had not been as successful, he had always adhered to this concept. He said in a low voice, "So you don't think there's value in building something that lasts?"

Olivia dipped her brush in a vivid yellow paint, contrasting with the muted background of her canvas. She answered, "There is value in living in the moment." She emphasized the importance of embracing the present moment. We shouldn't use love, relationships, and the arts as shackles to impose predetermined standards on ourselves. They should be untamed and unrestrained. As he observed her, Ethan's mind was racing. He respected Olivia's independence and her capacity to live so freely and fearlessly. However, it also frightened him. What if, according to her, this relationship they were developing was really a passing phase? What if she viewed their time together as merely another phase in her ever-changing life while he was beginning to feel something more profound? Every day the ambiguity intensified his doubts.

A few days later, Lucas's well-known face appeared in the town. After hearing about Ethan's creative retreat, an old buddy of Ethan's had travelled upstate to visit and catch up. The scent of freshly brewed coffee filled the room as they took their seats for the breakfast.

As he sipped his coffee, Lucas raised an eyebrow and continued, "So, this Olivia." "It sounds like she's really annoyed with you." Lucas said.

Ethan ran a hand through his hair and laughed. You might say that, yes. She's... unique. She is unlike anyone I have ever met. She challenges my preconceived notions about things.

Lucas sensed a deeper presence and inclined forward. "However?"

Ethan paused, uncertain how to express what he was thinking. However, I'm unsure if we share any common ground. She believes that love and life are fleeting. She believes that enduring something is not necessary. I've always supported permanence and creating long-lasting things. I'm not sure how to make that work.

Lucas leaned back in his seat, his face contemplative. "Ethan, you've always been someone who finds significance in everything. Olivia is wild and free-spirited, so I can see why you find her fascinating. However, do you believe you could find contentment with someone who holds different beliefs than you? Is there someone who lacks interest in the type of enduring partnership you're pursuing?

Gazing into his coffee, Ethan let out a sigh. "I'm not sure. She gives me a sense of aliveness that I haven't had in years. However, I can't get rid of the sensation that I'm walking on shaky ground. What if everything fails?

Lucas nodded in a calm and composed manner. Building anything on unstable ground usually results in its collapse. Perhaps it's thrilling right now, but what will happen if the thrill wanes? Stability has always been important to you, Ethan. Just because things feel different doesn't mean you should lose sight of what you truly desire. On some level, Ethan knew Lucas was correct. Security, the assurance that something will endure, had always been important to him. However, Olivia seemed to thrive amidst the chaos.

He was momentarily liberated from the burden of permanence. But did he find that sufficient? Could he truly create a future with someone who didn't hold the same values as him in terms of commitment and love?

Ethan ended up back at Olivia's studio later that night. Canvases in varying states of completion lined the walls, and the scent of paint and turpentine filled the tiny room. Olivia was working on a new painting while standing in the middle of the room, her hands moving swiftly. The painting's strong, flowing lines reflected the same wild energy that seemed to follow her everywhere.

Ethan observed her for a while before he began to speak. He said, "Do you ever wonder what happens when the moment is gone?" His thoughts weighed down his quiet voice. Olivia turned to face him as she wiped her hands with a rag. "What do you mean?"

The town, studio, and life they had lived for days were shown, and he asked, "I mean... what comes after all of this?" "After the exhilaration and rush? Do you ever yearn for something more enduring?

Ethan had never noticed the tenderness of Olivia's grin before. It was a more serious, reflective smile than the easygoing one she normally wore. In a soft voice, she remarked, "I don't think permanence makes something more meaningful." "Ethan, life is constantly changing. Situations and people change. I don't want to cling to something merely out of fear of losing it. It isn't living.

Her words pierced his heart, making him feel both terror and admiration. He admired her for being able to accept the turmoil and exist without the need for constant assurance. He wasn't like that, though. He required more. He needed a solid object to cling to, something he could trust. Lucas's words weighed heavily on him, reminding him of the dangers and the possible heartache.

"I simply..." Ethan began but was unable to finish. What he meant to express was unclear to him. Olivia took a step forward and met his gaze. She said, "You don't have to figure it all out right now." "We don't need to give everything a name. Let's simply be present and observe where this leads us.

Ethan nodded, but he couldn't shake the doubt. He wasn't sure whether he could live like her or like that. With every day that went by, the internal struggle intensified, dragging him in two different directions. The yearning for something tangible and long-lasting and the steadiness he had always cherished were on one side. Olivia, a tornado of passion and erratic behavior, was on the other side, promising him an exciting but uncertain life.

He had no idea which way to go. Additionally, he found it more difficult to make a decision the more time he spent with Olivia.

CHAPTER THREE- CREATIVE SYNERGY

The days passed swiftly, filled with a flurry of words and color. Warm light poured through Olivia's studio's tall windows, bathing the chaotic area that had become Ethan's haven. The scent was a combination of canvas, turpentine, and a subtle trace of lavender from the candles Olivia often burned while working. With his fingers hovering over the keyboard, Ethan sat at the tiny desk she had made room for him, his manuscript's blank page gradually filled with new words.

This unexpected surge of invention, this stream of ideas that would not stop, was unlike anything he had ever experienced when it came to writing. The pressure to produce anything substantial had paralyzed him for weeks, leaving him stuck in a circle of doubt. However, the words flowed effortlessly to him here in the studio with Olivia, as if their energy had unlocked a portal within him.

Olivia had a lot going on. Her whole body seemed to come alive with the beat of creation each time she picked up a brush. The colors on her canvas danced in chaotic harmony as she painted freely, her movements unfettered. Ethan found himself captivated by her as a person and as an artist. It was intoxicating—her passion, her freedom. However, something always stopped him, just as he thought they were getting into a rhythm. He wasn't sure he could overcome the invisible emotional barrier Olivia maintained.

He initially tried to ignore it, convincing himself that their shared artistic connection was sufficient. However, Ethan found himself becoming increasingly conflicted as the days passed. His desire to comprehend the more profound aspects of her, the pieces she concealed beneath the surface, grew as their creative relationship deepened. However, Olivia appeared to object to any attempts to explain their relationship.

Olivia's voice interrupted his thoughts. "Hey." She stood at the easel, brush in hand, giving him the sly smirk she always had when she saw him nodding off. "What's going through your mind?"

The cursor on his laptop flickered after a phrase as Ethan looked down at it. He lied and said, "I'm just trying to figure out where this character is going."

His character was not on his mind. She was on his mind. He wondered how she could seem so honest and alive yet remain a mystery to him. For days, he had been observing her in He made an attempt to understand her rhythm and procedure. However, each time he believed he understood her, she would do something that caused him to doubt everything.

She returned her attention to her painting and remarked, "I'm sure you'll figure it out." "You always do."

There was a hint of irritation in Ethan's smile. He had no desire to identify a character. He sought to understand Olivia.

Once more, the studio became silent, save for the occasional click of Ethan's keyboard and the gentle swish of Olivia's brush on canvas. They had established a cozy routine—an implicit understanding that they would collaborate without interfering with one another's work. It was a natural chemistry, and Ethan discovered that writing became easier the more time they spent together.

Olivia's unpredictable energy seemed to permeate his words. He no longer hesitated to experiment with his writing or to defy conventions. Olivia's artwork infused his sentences with the same vitality. Ethan felt alive in his work for the first time in months.

However, his emotions became entangled as his inventiveness flourished. He sensed a pull each time Olivia smiled at him and her fingertips touched his arm as she went by. He made an effort to ignore it, telling himself it was simply the thrill of collaboration. He felt in his heart that it was more than that, though. No one he had ever known was like Olivia. She forced him to consider things he had previously taken for granted. He felt unstable, despite his admiration for her.

After working in silence for a few hours one afternoon, Olivia put down her brush and took a moment to look at her painting. It was a whirling ball of color, vibrant and alive. Wiping her hands with a cloth, she turned to face Ethan.

As she approached him, she said, "You've been quiet today." "By now, you're usually typing like a crazy person."

Ethan raised his head and scanned her face. She seemed to be waiting for him to initiate contact because of the way she looked at him—so open, so inquisitive, but still cautious.

He spoke carefully, searching for the right words. "I've been thinking about us." Regarding this—whatever it is.

Olivia didn't turn away, but her smile dimmed a little. "What do you mean?"

Ethan hesitated, feeling as though his own doubt was weighing him down. "Isimply... I have no idea where we're headed." I'm not sure if we're in this together or just two people working.

Olivia looked away, as though gathering her thoughts, and her expression softened. "Is something more required?"

Her words made Ethan's heart sink a little, but he made himself keep on. "I'm not sure. I suppose we simply seem to have a connection that extends beyond art. However, I'm unsure whether you share my sentiments.

Olivia remained silent for a while as she twisted the rag between her hands without paying attention. When she did speak, it was in a quiet, almost wary tone. "Yes, Ethan, I do sense something. If I didn't, I wouldn't be here with you.

A glimmer of hope ignited in Ethan's heart as his chest constricted. "Then why do you appear to be holding back?" Are you afraid to let this escalate beyond its current state?

He couldn't quite interpret the range of emotions in Olivia's eyes as they methis. "I'm not scared," she murmured softly. "I simply don't think things should have labels. I don't think it's necessary to try to define something that doesn't exist. We have arrived. Isn't that sufficient?

Ethan swallowed forcefully, his annoyance rising to the surface. "What if I don't find it sufficient?"

Ethan noticed for the first time a glimmer of vulnerability in Olivia's eyes as her face wavered. Olivia's voice was barely audible as she stepped closer. "I don't want to lose our possessions. I'm not implying that I have no feelings for you. I simply don't want to try to make it something it's not, as it could ruin our relationship.

Ethan gazed at her, caught between the closeness he felt and the increasing awareness that their approaches to relationships were essentially different. He desired something tangible and enduring. Olivia, however, seems content to let things unfold without worrying about the future and to live in the now.

Finally, Ethan remarked, "I don't want to ruin it either." "But I'm not sure how long I can keep doing this—acting like we're just drifting."

Olivia gave a nod, her eyes falling to the ground. "I understand, Ethan. Yes, I do. But I am this person. I am unable to guarantee you anything beyond what we already have.

The ensuing silence weighed them down with unresolved tension. Ethan was devastated to learn that, despite his best efforts, Olivia would not provide him with the assurance he so desperately sought. Nevertheless, he was unable to go. Not quite yet. Their creative relationship was too strong and energizing to give up.

He got up and moved toward her, speaking in a stern yet gentle tone. "I suppose I'll have to determine whether or not that's sufficient for me."

Olivia searched his face as she stared up at him. Although she remained silent, how she maintained eye contact with him conveyed all the information he required. Even if it was indefinable, there was something genuine between them.

Their creative synergy remained strong as they worked side by side in quiet for the remainder of the afternoon. Throughout the day, Ethan felt like he was wandering between the excitement of their connection and the worry that it might never grow.

Ethan turned to face Olivia, who was once again absorbed in her painting as the sun started to drop and the studio's light faded. He was impressed by her technique—the way she seemed to put her all into each brushstroke. Under that respect, however, was a developing uneasiness—a feeling that their emotional trajectories might never fully coincide, regardless of how close they were creatively.

And when the feelings he couldn't deny finally demanded more than Olivia was prepared to provide, Ethan questioned whether the art they were making together would be enough to support him for the first time since he had moved to this little, quiet town.

The chapter concluded with the two of them working together in perfect harmony, just as it had begun. However, beneath that peace, Ethan sensed a deeper pull that threatened to upset the

  delicate equilibrium they had discovered.

Furthermore, he was uncertain as to how long he could ignore it.

Chapter Four- Push and Pull

Ethan had always thought that things become clearer with time and that your sentiments became more firmly established the longer you were with someone. Olivia, however, had the opposite situation. The longer he spent with her, the more perplexed he became. Each intimate encounter and connection seemed to intensify their hesitation.

Ethan felt alive in ways he hadn't experienced in years because of the creative energy and unstated rhythm that pervaded their days together. He was unable to adequately describe the rawness and flow that had come to his writing. Olivia's mere presence seems to have triggered something within him. The free-flowing words weren't the only thing, though. He felt both elated and profoundly uneasy, as his feelings were now exposed and vulnerable.

On one of those long evenings in the studio, everything culminated. For hours, they had been working together in silence, only broken by the faint tapping of Ethan's fingers and the sound of Olivia's brush moving over canvas. Beyond the familiar creative energy, a more electric energy charged the atmosphere, something neither of them seemed eager to confront directly.

Ethan could not deny the draw that was growing inside of him toward Olivia. He had tried to ignore it and focus on work, but their tension had become intolerable. Every time she moved, every time she looked at him, every time her arm touched his, he felt cold. The unspoken attraction that had been simmering beneath the surface since they first met was something he knew she felt as well. Nevertheless, she maintained emotional and physical distance, as if the only way to remain in control was to distance oneself.

However, something was different tonight. The air felt heavy, as if they were on the brink of something neither could exactly describe.

With a sigh of satisfaction, Olivia stepped back from her latest creation and wiped her hands on a rag. Olivia's hair tangled in an untidy knot on top of her head, her face flushed. She gave Ethan a quick glance and grinned—that recognizable, sly smile that always seemed to arouse something deep within him.

She murmured softly, "You've been quiet," yet there was a trace of something unsaid in her tone.

Ethan's heart was racing when he looked up from his laptop. He knew he couldn't ignore the unspoken messages between them tonight, as he could feel their weight. "Yes, I have been thinking."

"About what?" she asked as she walked over to the desk where he was sitting.

Ethan paused, trying to find the proper words. He had always exercised caution around Olivia, not wanting to push her too hard or be the one to ask for more than she was prepared to provide. However, he couldn't keep claiming that their attraction was solely based on their creative talents.

Finally, in a firm but quiet voice, he said, "About us." "Something like this."

Olivia's eyes flickered with an unidentified emotion, possibly dread, and her smile faltered. As though preparing for what was about to happen, she crossed her arms over her chest and leaned on the edge of the desk.

She began to say, "Ethan," but he interrupted her.

He got up to confront her and said, "Just listen to me." " I can't act like it's just about the work anymore; I have no idea what's going on between us. I have a genuine feeling for you. I believe you sense it as well, but you always back off when I approach.

When Olivia's eyes fell to the ground, Ethan briefly feared that she would turn and leave the studio, leaving him standing there with his heart on his sleeves. Instead, she inhaled deeply and raised her gaze to his, her eyes brimming with a range of feelings that he was unable to fully comprehend.

She whispered, "I do feel something for you, Ethan." I'm not like you, though. My perspective on relationships differs from yours. I cannot bind myself to anyone.

Her comments caused Ethan's chest to constrict. Although he had heard her say it previously, it sounded different and more genuine now. They were no longer merely discussing theoretical concepts. They were discussing one another.

His frustration surged as he replied, "I'm not asking you to be tied down." " I only want you to be honest with me. If you want things to stay exactly as they are at this moment, express it clearly. However, don't keep drawing me in only to push me out again.

Ethan was surprised by the sadness in Olivia's eyes as she gazed at him. "It's not that easy," she muttered. "I don't know how to handle this, but I don't mean to hurt you. I've never been excellent at letting people in or having relationships. I've tried, but it's always ended horribly. I don't want us to experience that. Ethan took a step toward them, bringing them closer. He could feel her warmth inches away, and his heart raced. With a voice that was almost audible above a whisper, he murmured, "Then stop pushing me away."

For a brief moment, everything seemed to be in the balance. Olivia gazed up at him, breathing heavily, her eyes fixed on his. Abruptly, she reached up and planted a gentle yet forceful kiss on his mouth. As he kissed her back and moved his hands to her waist to draw her in, Ethan's heart pounded in his chest.

After weeks of cultivating a relationship, it was a moment of unadulterated passion. While losing themselves in each other, the world seemed to disappear, and their tension broke in the most personal way. However, Olivia withdrew as quickly as the situation had begun. She stepped back, her eyes wide with what appeared to be fright and her breath ragged.

She shook her head and murmured, "I can't." "This is not something I can do."

Ethan's chest heaved as he stared at her, his mind racing with uncertainty. "What do you mean?"

Olivia retreated even more, her hands shaking. "I can't be what you want me to be," I told you. Ethan, I can't do this. Even if I believed I could, I couldn't accomplish this.

Ethan seemed to have torn the ground out from under him. "You're not even giving us a chance, Olivia. Why do you fear this so much?

Her expression hardened as she blinked away the tears that filled her eyes. "I don't want to lose myself in it." I've witnessed the results of attempts to make anything permanent. It crumbles. I will not allow myself to experience that.

Stunned by the abrupt change, Ethan stood there with his head spinning. She was withdrawing once more, retiring within the barriers she had erected around herself, although he had felt so close to her at that precise moment.

"Is that it then?" he asked in a hollow voice. "Every time things become real, are you going to continue running?"

Olivia took a while to respond. Her face was filled with turmoil as she gazed at him. Her voice was quiet as she said, "I don't want to hurt you.

"How can I meet your needs, though?"

A lump rose in Ethan's throat, but he forced it down. Olivia, I don't need you to be anything different from who you are. But I can't continue pushing and pulling like this. It's shredding me to pieces.

Ethan could tell that his words were insufficient to change her decision, yet she nodded slowly. She couldn't fully allow him in because she was too terrified and deeply rooted in her own fear of losing herself.

She muttered, "I'm sorry," and then turned to leave the studio, leaving Ethan standing by himself in the faint light of the room they had shared.

For what seemed like hours, Ethan stood there with his emotions in disarray and his mind racing. What to do and whether to continue this cycle of disappointment and hope was unknown to him. Though emotionally unpredictable, strong, and impenetrable, Olivia had become such an essential part of his artistic life.

Even though it left him feeling more out of balance than ever, Ethan recognized that this emotional rollercoaster was nourishing his work as he sat by himself at his computer that night and stared at the flickering cursor on his screen. The words that poured out of him, unfiltered and raw, reflected the bewilderment, the pain, and the hunger that had taken root in his heart.

However, while he spoke, a question kept coming to him: How long could he endure this ambiguous state, torn between the need for something tangible and the worry that it would never be sufficient? Even though he didn't know the answer, the uncertainty weighed down on him more and more as the night went on.

For the first time, he wasn't sure if he could handle it.

Chapter Five - Fractured Perspective

The sun formed long shadows over the trees as the road wound over the hills and valleys in front of them. They drove with the windows down, Olivia behind the wheel, her hair blowing in the breeze, the buzz of the engine mingling with the indie music on the radio. Watching her giggle while her hand tapped the steering wheel in rhythm with the music, Ethan sat in the passenger seat. She appeared carefree and at ease, and Ethan briefly let himself feel the same way. Olivia had conceived the spontaneous idea two days earlier, and they were en route to a nearby art market.

The fair, she clarified, was an assembly of unrestrained artists and makers, a location where individuals could immerse themselves in their work without societal constraints. Even while Ethan was eager to see what it would be like, he couldn't help but feel uneasy because it sounded like the kind of place Olivia would flourish. Since the night in the studio, when Olivia withdrew from him during a vulnerable moment, the tension between them has remained unchanged. The emotional distance between them had only widened despite Ethan's best efforts to ignore it and concentrate on their job and creative energies. He couldn't help but wonder as they raced toward the fair whether Olivia was using this excursion as a means of diverting their attention from the more serious problems that had been seething beneath the surface. Ethan's uneasiness increased as they arrived in the little, artistic village where the fair was taking place.

Vibrant murals, pop-up shops selling handcrafted items, and people wearing loose clothing lined the streets, in keeping with the place's free-spirited atmosphere. When Olivia parked the car, a group of artists putting up their stalls greeted her with grins and excited waves as soon as they got out.

She grabbed Ethan's hand and dragged him toward the main square, saying, "Come on." "You should meet some people," I said. Ethan surrendered to the guidance, yet his unease intensified as they traversed the fair. It was impossible for him to avoid feeling alienated in this world. People who appeared disconnected from the things that had always been important to him—commitment, stability, and structure—were all around him. Similar to Olivia, these artists crafted ephemeral works intended for immediate experience and subsequent forgetting, embracing the present moment. However, Ethan had always believed that art should endure, that it should endure the passage of time, just like love.Olivia gave him a charming smile in return, as if sensing his hesitancy. "Are you okay?" she inquired, her eyes glimmering with anticipation.

Ethan forced a smile and added, "Yeah." "I'm doing fine. This is... distinct. Olivia smiled, obviously energized by the surroundings. That's the main idea. It's going to be fantastic. They wandered from booth to booth for the next hour, pausing to talk to different creators and artists. Olivia was having a wonderful time joking and laughing with everyone she encountered. Her lively enthusiasm was contagious. Ethan made an effort to participate, but the more time he spent in this realm, the more alienated he felt. Like Olivia, these folks were free from the expectations that seemed to burden him so much. A woman with long silver hair was showing off abstract artworks created from driftwood, shards of broken glass, and rusted metal at one booth. Her voice was warm and affectionate as she greeted Olivia with an embrace. "Darling Olivia! The woman turned to Ethan and smiled curiously, saying, "I've missed you." "And who is this?" Olivia put a hand on Ethan's arm and murmured, "This is him." "He writes." "A writer?"

The woman had a glint in her eyes. "I adore authors. They always wind up in their hearts, even if they reside in their heads. Unsure of how to react, Ethan smiled courteously. After examining him for a while, the woman looked back at Olivia. "Are you two, then?" Her smile was lighthearted as she allowed the question to linger. Olivia waved her hand dismissively as she laughed. "Oh, no. We're simply—well, it's difficult. Ethan's stomach knotted at her comment, despite his best efforts to hide it. The woman noticed the unease, and her grin wavered. She answered tactfully, "Well, whatever it is, it's beautiful." "Enjoy the fair." Olivia's casual rejection of their love still stung Ethan as they left. He was aware that she hadn't intended to harm him. They were growing apart, but her ease in dismissing what they had widened the gap.

They made a lunch stop at a food truck and sat on the edge of a fountain to eat. After viewing all the fresh concepts at the show, Olivia was still full of energy as she talked about the artists they had met and the art she wished to produce. Ethan nodded in agreement as he listened, but his mind was elsewhere. Olivia commented, nudging him with her elbow. "You're quiet." Ethan grated his teeth. "Just pondering." "How about?" Before he could stop himself, he blurted out,

"About us." Olivia didn't back down, but her smile dimmed a little. "How about us?" Ethan put his sandwich down and used a napkin to wipe his hands. "I'm not sure. I suppose I'm merely attempting to ascertain our current position. With a sigh, Olivia leaned back against the fountain and looked over the crowd. "We've discussed this, Ethan." With a hint of annoyance in his voice, he added, "I know." However, I'm still making an effort to understand. I have no idea how to survive in this limbo. Despite our differences, we sense a connection. Although we are together, we are not truly together. I simply have no idea what you desire. Olivia remained silent for a while, her eyes averted.

Her voice was forceful yet gentle when she eventually spoke. "Ethan, I refuse to feel bound. I've been telling you that since day one. As his fury grew, Ethan remarked, "I'm not asking you to be tied down." " All I'm asking is that you tell me what this is, honestly. I'm uncertain whether your distance from me is due to fear or a lack of empathy for my feelings. Olivia's countenance was troubled as she gazed at him. "Yes, Ethan, you are important to me. A wonderful deal. I'm not like you, though. Things don't have to be permanent or definite for me to feel real. "That's the issue," Ethan stated in a tense tone. "I do." I cannot continue to act as though this is sufficient for me when it is not. Ethan almost believed Olivia might reach out to him and give him some sort of comfort as her eyes softened. Rather, she shook her head, her face dejected. "I'd rather not lose you," she said. "But I don't want to change myself to cheer you up." Her comments made Ethan's heart sink. He was aware of her correctness. Despite her honesty from the beginning, accepting it didn't come any easier. In reality, he was falling for her—in fact, he had fallen in love—but he couldn't ignore their fundamental differences.

Olivia was unencumbered by commitment or expectations and lived in the present. Ethan, however, required something more. Their relationship changed as they walked around the fair all afternoon. A thick silence with sporadic word exchanges had replaced the playful banter and shared enthusiasm. Olivia attempted to defuse the tension by making light of it, but it only made matters worse. Ethan was too preoccupied with his thoughts and too conscious of their increasing separation.

The sun was starting to set by the time they left the fair and made their way back to the car, leaving the surrounding area in lengthy shadows. Ethan glanced out the window, buried in his own anguish, as Olivia drove in quietly, her face unreadable. Olivia finally spoke, her voice calm yet quiet, as they drew into the driveway of her studio. She turned off the engine and turned to face Ethan, saying, "I don't want to hurt you." "However, I can't be what you desire." A knot formed in Ethan's throat, but he swallowed it and nodded slowly. His voice was hardly audible above a whisper when he added, "I know." "I'm not sure if I can continue doing this."

Olivia tentatively but gently reached for his hand. "Perhaps we will need some time to resolve this." Ethan's heart ached as he gazed at her. Even though he knew she was right, accepting it didn't come any easier. He became increasingly aware of how much he cared for her the more time they spent together. However, he also realized that their basic differences might be too significant to overcome. At last, he murmured in a voice laden with resignation, "I suppose we do." As they sat in the car, their fractured perspectives weighing heavily on them, Ethan couldn't help but wonder if this was the beginning of the end. He was also doubtful about their first reunion since meeting.

Chapter Six - Confessions

The dimly illuminated bar was filled with the sound of clinking glasses and the spinning of old records. Olivia sat opposite Ethan, her face glowing in the dim candlelight. The scent of wood and whiskey permeated the air, and the faint jazz music coming from the corner blended with the quiet murmur of discussion. Their decision to travel here, like many of their excursions, was impromptu and sprang from the underlying tension that had developed between them since their road trip to the art market. Ethan had no idea how this had happened.

Numerous times, he had hoped that they would eventually be able to get past their wall, but Olivia always retreated, keeping him at a distance. He had thought that tonight they would find solace in the familiar, in their mutual appreciation of art, and in their capacity to become absorbed in conversation. However, the burden of all he had been suppressing became too heavy to handle after a few too many beers. He observed Olivia sipping her beverage while her fingers idly traced the glass's rim. Ethan wondered if Olivia felt the same weight he did—the same tug between wanting to be closer and being terrified of what that might entail, given that she was quieter than usual tonight.

Ethan remarked, his voice hoarse from the booze, "I've been thinking a lot." Olivia's eyes, steady but wary, looked up. "How about?" "Concerning us." Before he could stop them, the words poured out of him, and whatever he had been suppressing seemed to be coming to the surface. We're discussing the nature of this situation and our actions here. We frequently discuss the same topic, yet we rarely express it explicitly. Olivia's face changed a little, but she said nothing more, waiting for him to go on. Ethan took a deep breath, letting the warmth of the wine loosen his inhibitions.

His voice was firm but gentle as he replied, "I'm falling for you, Olivia." I don't know where I stand with you, but I've been getting into you. I feel like I'm waiting for you to push me away or let me in, like I'm walking a tightrope. Olivia didn't respond right away; her eyes briefly strayed before returning to his. Her face was unreadable, and the ensuing silence was oppressive, as if it were crushing against Ethan's chest. At last, she said quietly, "I'm not sure what you want me to say." Ethan felt anger rising within him and shook his head. Olivia, you don't have to say anything. All I ask is that you tell me the truth. Do you want this to be real, or am I alone? With a sigh, Olivia put down her glass and combed through her hair.

She appeared worn out, as though she had been toting a heavy object for too long. "Ethan, it's not that easy." "Why isn't it?" he asked, his voice tinged with frustration. "You're with me here. You never let it go beyond the fact that we spend so much time together and connect on so many levels. What's causing your fear? Olivia closed her eyes for a time, and when she opened them, something flickered beneath the surface, either dread or agony. She whispered, "I don't fear you." "I'm worried about What could happen if this situation escalates beyond its current state? I have witnessed the results of people's attempts to make things last. It never ends well. Ethan's forehead wrinkled, his chest churning with uncertainty and pain. "What are you discussing?"

Olivia inhaled deeply while tracing patterns on the table with her fingertips, seemingly in an attempt to arrange her thoughts. "My parents," she said, sounding as if she were speaking from someone else. "They loved each other with such passion and intensity. However, it was also harmful. In the end, everything broke apart despite their best efforts to make it work and create something durable. I saw them harming and destroying one another until nothing remained. She stopped and looked down at her hands. "I vowed to myself that I would not allow that to occur. I would not allow myself to fall victim to anything that could potentially destroy me. Her comments made Ethan's heart hurt.

The memory of her parents' broken relationship had influenced her perspective of the world, and he could see the anguish in her eyes. It clarified a lot of the reasons she opposed attempts at permanence and maintained a distance from him and everyone else. "I'm not your parents, Olivia," he murmured. "We don't have to experience what happened to them." With a conflicted expression, she shook her head. "Ethan, you don't understand. You want something genuine and long-lasting, but I'm not sure how to provide it. I've never excelled in building relationships. I'm uncertain about how to meet your needs. Ethan took her hand in his as he reached across the table. "You just need to be yourself; I don't require you to be anything else. However, I can't pretend that I don't yearn for more. I want to spend more time with you than just these few minutes. I'm looking for something genuine. Olivia's eyes strayed to their hands, her fingers quivering a little under his hold. She muttered, "I don't know if I can give that to you." "I'm not sure if I can be who you want me to be without becoming someone else."

Ethan struggled to maintain his composure while his heart fell. "Olivia, I'm not requesting that you lose yourself. All I'm seeking is permission to enter. More than I've cared for anyone in a long time, I care about you. However, I must ascertain whether you will ever experience the same emotion. Olivia didn't answer for a second. She seemed to be grappling with an issue that Ethan couldn't penetrate. At last, she raised her gaze to him, sorrow shining in her eyes. She whispered, "Ethan, I also care about you." "I do." However, I'm not sure if I can provide you with what you're requesting. What happens when things get serious scares me. I'm afraid I'll get hurt.

Ethan's chest ached from a mixture of aggravation and empathy as his hold on her hand tightened a little. "Everyone fears injury," he said. However, that does not imply that you should deny the possibility of something genuine. I realize it's frightening, but often the most exciting things in life are also the most frightening. Olivia gave a small smile that stopped short of her eyes. She said, "I wish I could see it the way you do." "But I've witnessed too much to think that kind of enduring happiness is possible." Her remarks caused a slight break in Ethan's heart. He wanted to think that he could make her reconsider, that she may lower her defenses if he simply showed her how much he cared. However, as they conversed, he became increasingly aware that Olivia's dread was more profound than he had initially thought. It was about all she had ever known, not just about them. "So, what do we do?" Ethan asked in a passionate voice. "Where do we go from there?" Olivia looked at him with a saddened face. "I'm not sure," she muttered. "Ethan, I don't want to lose you. Actually, I don't. However, I'm unsure if I can fulfill your requirements.

Ethan's throat constricted, preventing him from speaking for a while. He didn't want to abandon Olivia or miss out on their potential together. However, he was also aware that he couldn't continue to live in this state of uncertainty, torn between heartbreak and hope. At last, his voice cracked a little as he remarked, "I don't know if I can keep doing this." Olivia, I need more than just these moments with you, but I still want to be with you. I need to believe that we have a bright future together. Olivia hurriedly pushed away the tears that welled up in her eyes.

She said, "I don't want to hurt you." "But I can't commit to anything that I'm not sure I can follow through on."Ethan gazed at her, the weight of all that remained unsaid pressing down on his heart. He knew he couldn't compel her to realize that they could be more than this, but he still wanted to fight for her. Olivia needed to realize that herself, but she wasn't ready yet.Olivia spoke in a tremulous voice, "Perhaps you don't have to promise anything." "Perhaps we could simply be present and observe where it leads." Her comments caused Ethan's chest to constrict.

He desired to think that he could accept whatever Olivia was prepared to offer and live in the moment. He knew in his heart that he required more than that, though. It was important to him that this was not a temporary phase.With a regretful tone, Ethan muttered, "I'm not sure if I can do that." I'm not sure I can wait for something that may never happen."Although Olivia's expression dimmed, she nodded, realizing the significance of what he had said. "I apologize," she muttered. "I wish I could be someone else." I wish I could provide for your needs. A knot formed in Ethan's throat, but he made himself look at her. "I hope You might as well," he remarked quietly. As they sat across from one another in the dark bar light, Ethan came to the realization that, despite his deep affection for Olivia, they were on different sides of a bridge that neither of them could cross.

CHAPTER SEVEN- FRIEND'S VISIT

Ethan sat on his apartment's front stairs and watched the leaves fall from the trees that bordered the street without paying any attention. Gazing down the deserted road, he could feel the coolness seeping into the early fall air beneath his skin. He wasn't sure if it was a blessing or a weight, but the silence that had descended on him since Olivia hadn't contacted since their night at the pub felt quite heavy. At the same time, he was afraid of what he might learn from that conversation, but he also wanted to reach out and close the gap between them.

He turned to see Lucas walking toward him, his hands tucked into his jacket pockets, a warm smile tugging at the edges of his mouth as he heard footsteps approaching. Life in the city had a way of keeping people apart, so it had been a while since Ethan had seen his old friend, but even though Ethan hadn't specifically asked for it, he could always rely on Lucas to be there for him when he needed him most.

Lucas walked over and raised an eyebrow in his sly manner, saying, "You look like you've been thinking too much."

With a shrug, Ethan got up to meet him. "I guess I have a lot on my mind."

Lucas looked at him sharply. "I assumed. That's the reason I'm here.

They were seated at the little café down the street, a well-known location that had witnessed many of the chats between Ethan and Lucas over the years. The aroma of warm pastries and freshly brewed coffee filled the air, providing a moment's relief from the stress that had been plaguing Ethan for weeks. After placing their order and exchanging pleasantries, the topic of conversation quickly turned to what had been bothering Ethan.

Lucas leaned back in his chair, scrutinizing his companion, and asked, "So?" "What's happening between Olivia and you?"

With a groan, Ethan combed through his hair. "It's difficult."

"Isn't it always? Lucas laughed, but it was in a serious rather than humorous tone. But really, dude, you seem a little strange. What's happening?"

Ethan paused. Since he had met Olivia, he had been struggling with a jumble of feelings, and he wasn't sure how to begin to describe them. He felt alive in her presence, but he also felt like he was always on precarious ground because of the tug and the unpredictability. He inhaled deeply and began at the beginning, explaining to Lucas how they had first met and how their artistic synergy had grown into something more profound, but that it always seemed like there was a barrier separating them that he was unable to go beyond.

As Ethan went on, Lucas listened intently, occasionally nodding and furrowing his brow. Lucas leaned forward and rested his elbows on the table when Ethan finally reached the section about Olivia's fear of commitment and her unwillingness to provide him with the surety he so desperately wanted.

"You have to ask yourself if this is truly what you want, Ethan," he added in a kind yet forceful voice. I understand; Olivia seems amazing, and you seem to genuinely care about her. However, it sounds like the entire situation is tearing you apart.

Naturally protective, Ethan scowled. "I'm not sure. It's not that easy.

But isn't it? Lucas raised an eyebrow in question. "Look, I understand that relationships can be challenging, but there's a distinction between conquering challenges and enduring a perpetual state of uncertainty." You have been telling me how great she is, but you also have been telling me how hard it is because she cannot meet your needs.

Ethan started to reply, but Lucas interrupted him by raising a hand.

Lucas went on, "I'm not saying you shouldn't care about her, and I'm not saying she doesn't care about you." However, you've always valued consistency and want something substantial and long-lasting. Based on everything you've told me, Olivia doesn't seem to be able to provide you with that. I'm concerned that the intensity of it all is consuming you.

A knot of resentment tightened in Ethan's chest as he reacted angrily to Lucas' remarks. What are you saying, then? That I ought to simply leave? Because she's afraid to commit, give up on her!"

With a calm but firm tone, Lucas stated, "I'm not saying you should walk away." Consider your true desires and whether Olivia will ever be able to fulfill them. Although chemistry and passion are wonderful, they are not the same as a foundation. The question is whether you are living in the moment or creating something lasting.

Ethan's mind was racing as he glanced down at his coffee. Lucas's comments resonated deeply, despite his reluctance to acknowledge them. He had been struggling with the same issues himself, questioning whether his intense feelings for Olivia were impairing his judgment. But when they were together, everything else seemed to fade away. However, the truth of their differences struck him hard, reminding him that despite his love for her, they might never share the same desires.

At last, Ethan remarked in a hushed voice, "I don't know." "I simply don't know."

Leaning back in his chair, Lucas looked at Ethan with a mixture of empathy and worry. "I realize you don't want to let go, but don't let it consume you. You need to be honest with yourself about how sustainable this is. You're looking for something tangible and lasting. What will happen to you if Olivia is unable to provide it?

Ethan's jaw tightened as Lucas's comments began to sink in. Since Olivia had acknowledged she couldn't guarantee him anything that night at the pub, he had been asking himself the same question for weeks. He had made an effort to ignore it, to persuade himself that perhaps he could live in the present as she desired, but he knew deep down that this was not who he was. He required more than transient desire—more than moments. Something he could grasp was necessary.

"I understand," Ethan murmured softly, his tone resigned. "You're correct; I know that. It's simply difficult.

Lucas softened his tone and continued, "I know it's true." However, you also need to defend yourself. Avoid becoming so engrossed in her world that you neglect your own needs.

The conversation weighed on them as they sat quietly. Even though Lucas' candor hurt, Ethan valued it. Even if Ethan didn't want to hear it, he had always been the friend who could see things clearly and wasn't scared to give him the harsh facts.

Lucas eventually got up and gave Ethan a shoulder clap. "Look, dude, I'm not giving you instructions. Just give it some thought. Both happiness and a relationship with someone who can provide for your needs are things you deserve. Don't forget about that.

With a nod, Ethan got up to lead Lucas to the door. "I appreciate you stopping by. This was what I needed.

Lucas smiled reassuringly and said, "Anytime." "Please don't get too caught up in your thoughts. You will discover the solution.

As Lucas disappeared around the corner, Ethan watched him stroll down the street. Once Lucas was out of sight, Ethan turned and headed back to his apartment, the exchange still replaying in his mind.

Ethan knew Lucas was correct. He couldn't continue to wait for Olivia to provide him with the assurance he required, living in this uncertain zone all the time. The thought of leaving her—of abandoning the possibility of more—weighed on his chest.

Ethan sat by himself in his apartment that evening, gazing at the blank page on his laptop screen. His mind was too thick to ignore, too jumbled to write. He couldn't stop thinking about Olivia and how she simultaneously made him feel alive and shaky. He was unable to ignore the draw he felt for her or deny their chemistry. However, Lucas's remarks continued to repeat in his mind, serving as a constant reminder that stability and passion were not synonymous.

Ethan shut down his laptop, doubt weighing heavily on his mind. He was uncertain about his next course of action. He wasn't sure if he could wait for Olivia to let him in or not. He wasn't sure if he was ready to let her go.

For the first time, Ethan wasn't sure if he could handle the emotional risks he had been taking with Olivia. It was beginning to feel overwhelming, akin to an impending storm.

CHAPTER EIGHT- A MOMENTARY HIGH

The afternoon sun filtered through the foliage and created shifting shadows over the automobile as the tiny dirt road wound its way through the thick forest. Olivia sat beside him with her feet up on the dashboard, her eyes searching the terrain with a calm focus, while Ethan held onto the steering wheel as they ventured farther into the bush. They were traveling to a cabin that was miles away from everything and hidden in a remote valley by a lake. Olivia came up with the idea, making a snap decision to put their job first and escape the relationship-defining stress.

When she had suggested it, Ethan had not thought twice. He had hoped that perhaps they could find some clarity outside the city, away from the stress and uncertainty. When they got closer to their destination, he wasn't sure if being alone would bring them closer or widen the emotional gap. Olivia broke the stillness by stating, "I used to come out here all the time." "I used to come here when I needed to clear my head and reset." It's peaceful; you'll adore it. Ethan managed a tiny smile as he looked at her. "It's stunning."

Olivia returned the smile, but there was a wall that had existed in her eyes since their last talk. There was a sense of anticipation that something on this journey may rekindle the creative spark they had once shared, despite the animosity between them. Ethan believed that emotion and creativity intertwined, and despite his doubts, he couldn't ignore the strength of their creative bond. The cabin was rustic and basic, with wide windows overlooking the lake, just as Olivia had described it when they eventually got there. The air was cool and crisp, with a hint of dirt and pine in it, and the vista was breathtaking.

Olivia unlocked the door and stepped inside while Ethan waited on the porch, soaking it all in. From the living room, she exclaimed, "There is positive energy here." "I sense it already." Ethan walked slowly after her as he looked around the room. The room was compact yet comfortable, featuring an antique wooden table filled with art supplies seemingly untouched for years, a well-worn couch, and a wood-burning heater in one corner. Olivia was already settling in, arranging her paints beside the window and taking out her sketchbook. With a hint of the excitement he remembered from their first meeting, she turned to Ethan and said, "Let's start creating." "Avoid any interruptions. Only the work and us. With a jolt of excitement, Ethan nodded. Perhaps this time apart, an opportunity to concentrate on their craft without the burden of their emotional baggage, was just what they needed.

His fingers aching to type, he took out his laptop and placed it on the table. He hadn't had this inspiration in weeks, and he couldn't help but wonder whether being here with Olivia, away from everything else, would be the secret to releasing whatever had been preventing him from moving forward. A flurry of creative energy characterized the first several days. For hours on end, Ethan wrote, letting the words come out of him with a rawness he hadn't experienced in years. His writing was incisive, vulnerable, and full of passion, as though he had finally been able to release everything he had been suppressing.

Olivia also appeared to flourish in the seclusion. Her paintings were more expressive than he had ever seen, as she painted with such passion that they were overflowing with color and energy. Their relationship was stronger in silence than in words, and they rarely spoke, instead connecting via their art. For the first time in weeks, Ethan thought the air tension might be enough. He lost himself in the creative euphoria they had experienced together, letting go of the worries and questions that had troubled him.

They sat on the porch with a view of the lake one evening after a particularly demanding workday. The sky was a deep shade of blue, and the stars were just starting to come out. They passed the bottle of wine Olivia had opened back and forth in silence while Ethan gazed out at the lake, the warmth of the booze coursing through his muscles. After some time, Olivia quietly responded, "I needed this." "Working like this. Being here." Sometimes it's the only thing that makes sense to me.

After nodding and taking a sip of wine, Ethan returned the bottle to her. "I understand. In the last few days, I've written more than I have in months. It is pleasant. Olivia grinned, but her eyes showed longing, as if she was missing something. Her voice was hardly audible above a whisper as she declared, "This is what I want." "To live in this manner. To produce without any preconceived notions, without concern about its meaning or direction, is the goal. At what she said, Ethan's chest constricted, and the old pain of doubt returned. Olivia's words reminded her that this was it, even though he was trying to forget and lose himself in the present.

She only desired these short moments, fleeting highs, and no consideration of the future. Their shared artistic connection was sufficient for her. However, this was only a fraction of what Ethan required.It wasn't simply the art he desired. He wants the stability and permanence that come from knowing they were creating something together—something that would endure beyond the cabin, past the next book or painting. Olivia, however, didn't share that opinion. The more time he spent with her, the more he understood how different they were; she lived for now. Ethan briefly allowed himself to think that this passion, this creative synergy, may be enough to keep them going that night as they sat in the dark with the wine bottle empty between them. But he knew in his heart that it wasn't.

Their artistic connection was reaching new heights, but the emotional gap between them was widening. And he couldn't get rid of the notion that the high they had experienced was fleeting and that the inevitable crash was only a short distance away, despite his best efforts to cling to it. They resumed their routine the following morning, each absorbed in their own task. The people and their feelings in Ethan's book were reflecting his own in ways that seemed almost too real. Similar to him, his protagonist grappled with the tension between two realms: the fear of becoming lost in something fleeting and the yearning for something deep and lasting.Olivia appeared to be using the canvas to process her own feelings as well. Compared to her other paintings, her most recent one was darker, had more subdued colors, and had sharper lines. It seemed as though their conflict had crept into her writing and shown itself in ways that were impossible for either of them to ignore.

The creative energy that had kept them going started to change by the fourth day. The pleasant silence between them grew heavy as the fervor that once drove their art became overwhelming. Ethan sensed the growing gap and the questions that remained unsaid. Additionally, the words no longer flowed as naturally, even when he made an effort to lose himself in his work. The old weight of uncertainty was returning, and the high they had experienced was starting to wear off. Ethan finally broke the silence that night as they sat by the fireplace, only the flames crackling. Do you ever consider what might occur next?

His voice was quiet and almost hesitant as he inquired. Olivia's brow furrowed as she looked up from her sketchbook. "What are you saying?" Ethan struggled to find the perfect words as he said, "I mean, after the cabin, after the art." "What occurs if we return? When does the moment end?" Although Olivia's face relaxed, her eyes remained cautious. Why must you always know what's going to happen next? With a groan, Ethan combed through his hair. I need to know if we are heading in the right direction. Olivia, I can't stay in this state of uncertainty. I require more.

Olivia looked at him and put down her sketchbook. I'm uncertain about the message you're trying to convey, Ethan. I've previously stated that I'm not seeking a long-term relationship. I'm uncertain about how to fulfill that role for you. Ethan's chest constricted, and he was momentarily unsure of how to react. He thought this artistic getaway would bring them closer and help them decide. However, it was now evident that, despite their close relationship, they were still on different sides of the same divide. At last, Ethan remarked in a voice laden with resignation, "I know you're not." "However, I can't resist wanting more."

Olivia averted her gaze; her face hurt. "Ethan, I wish I could be that person for you." However, I am unable to alter who I am. After that, they sat in silence for a long time, the fire gradually going out while the gap between them widened even more. Ethan came to the realization that, despite his love for the highs they experienced together, they would never be sufficient to heal the emotional gap that separated them in that silence and the dying light of the flames. He also questioned how much longer he could continue to act the other way as the night went on.

Chapter Nine - Confrontation

Ethan and Olivia strolled through the town's winding streets in the fresh late autumn air, the cobblestones slippery from the light rain that had fallen earlier in the evening. It was quiet because the seasons had reduced visitor and resident activity. As they strolled, Ethan glanced at Olivia, who was holding her hands in her coat pockets with a detached demeanor. Since leaving the cabin earlier that day, they hadn't talked much, and the stillness between them was getting deeper by the minute.

Before their journey to the lodge, they had planned this dinner at a nearby café as a way to reconnect with the outside world after their extreme seclusion. However, as they neared the small, dimly lit café, a sense of dread began to creep into Ethan's spine. He could feel the tension building between them for weeks and knew something had to give tonight. The warm glow of the candle on the table created flickering shadows on Olivia's face as they took their seats in a corner booth by the window.

With its exposed brick walls and shelves stocked with antique books and trinkets, the café had a homey feel. It should have been comforting, but instead, many unspoken words were floating in the air between them. The hush persisted even after the waiter came and went, taking their orders and dropping them off with their beverages. As he sipped his wine, Ethan observed Olivia gazing out the window while she traced the lip of her glass with her fingers. He had been waiting for her to acknowledge their separation by saying something—anything at all.

Olivia, however, stayed withdrawn, as though she were in a completely different place. Finally, Ethan had reached his lowest point. His voice was stern but quiet as he stated, "We need to talk." Olivia glanced back at him and blinked once. "How about?" Ethan set down his glass and leaned forward, uttering the words "About Us." "About our current relationship." Olivia's face tightened as she moaned. "We've been through this before, Ethan." "No, we haven't," Ethan answered, his annoyance revealing itself.

We have been staying away from it. Avoiding it has been your strategy. Olivia's eyes flashed with either defensiveness or wrath. "What am I supposed to say? I've expressed my feelings to you. "That's the issue," Ethan stated, raising his voice a little. "You claim to care about me, but whenever we get close, you keep stepping back. You appear to be shielding yourself from your own emotions by expressing a need for "freedom" out of fear of revealing your vulnerability. Olivia's jaw tensed, and she put down her glass a bit more forcefully than was necessary. She yelled, "I'm not fleeing from anything." "No, I'm not hiding because I don't fit your relationship ideal." Ethan's annoyance boiled over as his chest constricted. Olivia, I'm not attempting to exert control over you.

Just let me know where I stand with you. You always retreat when I believe we're making progress. You stop talking. This constant tugging is not acceptable to me.Olivia leaned closer and spoke in a low, harsh voice as her eyes hardened. "You truly want control, but you believe you need more. Since there is no other way to feel protected, define and box it. But that's not my way of life, Ethan. I do not love that way. Her remarks made Ethan wince, but he didn't back down. "This isn't about control," he said, his voice strained.

It all comes down to wanting something tangible and lasting. You behave as though it were a prison, but it's not. It's about creating something solid and dependable together. Olivia shook her head, a look of incredulity on her face. "You're not getting it. Establishing roots and acting as if nothing will change is not love. You're scared of things coming apart; therefore, that's what you want. But, Ethan, things do go wrong. That's life. With his heart thumping in his ears, Ethan balled his fists beneath the table. So what? Our purpose is to focus solely on the present moment, without any concern for the future.

We should never care about the future. Olivia's voice was harsh as she answered, "Yes." "Why isn't that sufficient? Why can't we just be in the moment without trying to change it?" Ethan gazed at her, her words weighing heavily on his emotions. He was aware from the start that they were different and that Olivia held different beliefs than he did. But hearing her say it aloud, so brutally, felt like a knife twisting in his chest.Ethan's voice was hardly audible above a whisper as he continued, "I can't do that." "I can't live that way."

For a brief moment, Olivia's expression softened, and Ethan believed he caught a glimpse of sadness in her eyes. She shook her head, though, and her shields came up again in an instant. Then perhaps we're not meant to be together," she said. For a brief moment, Ethan was not able to breathe as the words struck him like a kick to the stomach. The fact that they were on different sides of a barrier that neither of them could cross terrified him. However, after listening to Olivia's admission that they might never be able to resolve this, he felt empty.

"So that's it? Ethan's voice trembled with emotion. "You're simply going to leave because it's simpler than attempting to resolve this?" Olivia's eyes flashed once more, but this time they were hurt and frustrated at the same time. "Ethan, I'm not going anywhere. But just because it makes you feel better doesn't mean I'm going to change who I am. I cannot become the person you desire me to be. Frustrated, Ethan replied, "I'm not asking you to change who you are." "I'm requesting that we meet halfway.

You must stop running whenever the situation becomes serious. Unshed tears filled Olivia's eyes as she shook her head. "Do you not understand? I am unable to fulfill your request. I can't stay bound to anything that confines me. I've been there before, and I won't be returning. Ethan began to argue, only to have his words cut off in his throat. Her dread and will to maintain her independence at any cost were evident in her eyes. That's when he realized that no matter how much he cared for her and how much he wanted to be with her, their desires would never align.The revelation swept over him like a wave, leaving him gasping for air.With a hollow voice, Ethan finally answered, "I don't know what else to say." Olivia, you are loved. However, I can't continue to live this way. I require more.

Olivia blinked back tears and turned her head away. She muttered, "I wish I could give that to you." "But I am unable to." The weight of their words hung between them in the deafening hush that followed. Ethan swallowed forcefully, attempting to control his emotions as a lump rose in his throat. To show her that they could succeed, he wanted to defend her. But he knew in his heart that Olivia had already decided what she wanted to do. There was no way she would change. He also couldn't keep requesting it from her. The distance between them felt larger than it had ever been as they sat there for a long time without saying anything to each other. Around them, the café had become silent, with the few people who were still there absorbed in their own chats and oblivious to the emotional turmoil rising at the corner table. At last, Olivia got up and draped her coat over her shoulder.

Her face was a mixture of resignation and despair as she gazed down at Ethan. "I will leave," she muttered. "I believe that both of us need some time to reflect." Unable to think of anything to say in response, Ethan nodded. With a gentle ding of the bell, he saw the door swing close behind Olivia as she turned and left the café. After she departed, he sat there for a while, gazing down at the empty spot where she had been, his heart heaving from the weight of all that remained unsaid. Ethan wasn't sure if he and Olivia could reconcile for the first time since he had met her. As he sat in the quiet, dimly lit café, he wondered if they ever should.

Chapter Ten - The Silent Rift

For Ethan, the days following the argument were like entering a strange, foreign universe. An unspoken gap now weighs down the once-unquestionable bond between him and Olivia. They were emotionally raw from the café altercation and retreated into their own corners to avoid discussing it again. Though everything had changed, Ethan still saw her. When they were together, they appeared cautious to avoid initiating the same conversation that had nearly led to their breakup. The weight of what they hadn't said made the cozy, friendly silence feel oppressive.

When she went by, Olivia still brushed her palm across his arm and smiled at him, but the warmth had diminished. Ethan wasn't sure if he could stop her from pulling away, let alone how. When life got too difficult to handle, he buried himself into his writing, like he usually did. The story suddenly accelerated after appearing to be stuck and aimless due to the chaos inside of him. His characters gained a new depth, their emotions and hardships reflecting his own in ways that seemed all too genuine. In the tiny nook of his flat, he would stay up late every night to pound away at his keyboard, his fingers rushing to keep up with the stream of words that spilled out of him. That was the only way he could comprehend Olivia's situation.

He felt as though he was writing every sentence and scene in a desperate attempt to understand the anguish and bewilderment that had gripped his heart. Like him, his protagonist was caught between two worlds: the worry that the person he loved would never be able to provide for him and the need for something profound and enduring. In contrast, Olivia seems to have lost herself in her artwork. She hadn't invited him, and Ethan hadn't visited her studio since they got back from the cabin. She painted all day, devoting herself to her task with an intensity that surpassed his own burst of creativity. Despite their physical proximity, there was a noticeable gap between them. Technically speaking, they were still together, but it felt like the basis of their previous relationship was collapsing under their feet. The stillness between them grew strained one evening as they sat together in her flat. Ethan didn't recognize the partially completed picture Olivia was working on at her easel.

Her brushstrokes were slower and more methodical, and the colors were muted and gloomy, unlike her typical vivid palette. Ethan was not writing as he sat on the couch with his laptop open on his knees. He was observing her, noting how her brow furrowed in focus and how her shoulders stiffened with each brushstroke. The words stuck in his throat as he tried to speak—to break the silence. What could be said? Since the argument, they had deliberately steered clear of any talk that would bring up the unanswered questions that still hung between them.

Olivia eventually put down her brush and turned to face him, her eyes weary. Is the writing progressing? Although she asked in an informal tone, there was a hint of stress in her voice. After hesitating, Ethan shut down his laptop. "It's good. I'm getting better. "That's fantastic," Olivia remarked in a bland voice. Although it didn't reach her eyes, she gave him a slight smile. "I'm happy." They fell back into stillness, the gap between them widening with each second that went by. Ethan wanted to contact her and ask her what was truly happening, but he was scared.

He was concerned that another altercation might push them over the edge. As a result, he remained silent and observed Olivia returning her attention to her painting. As the days passed in this manner, they both managed to avoid the inevitable. Ethan's excursions to Olivia's apartments became more irregular and remote, and he saw her less regularly than before. They seemed to be going through the motions while together, trying to hold onto something that was fading. A silent, nagging strain had taken the place of the passion that had once characterized their relationship.

Ethan gave his writing everything he had. It served as his only source of stability and a channel for feelings he was unable to communicate to Olivia. His book took on a life of its own, and the plot developed into something more nuanced and sinister than he had anticipated. The protagonist's journey reflected his psychological conflict, caught between the need for connection and the dread of losing himself in something that would never last. After writing for a while, Ethan sat at his desk late one night and gazed at the words on the computer. For the first time in days, he found it difficult to type, even though his fingers were hovering over the keyboard. The weight of his predicament with Olivia was bearing down on him more than ever, leaving him emotionally and creatively exhausted. He was unable to find a solution, but the stillness between them was getting intolerable.

Before the dispute, before the cabin, he reflected on the last time they had been very close. It had been simple for them to connect, and their creative synergy had brought them together in almost mystical ways. Now, doubt and uncertainty had taken the place of that magic. He sat on the edge of the desk and looked at his phone. Olivia had left a message, a straightforward "Hey, how's it going?" That seemed less like a sincere effort to get back in touch and more like a duty. His fingers lingered on the keyboard as he gazed at the screen, unsure of how to react. How could he respond? Did he miss her? He was unsure of how long they could continue to act as though nothing was wrong.

Rather, with the weight of his inaction pressing down on his chest, he closed the message and put the phone down. When Ethan woke up the following morning, the sun was shining through his window, but it didn't feel as close as it normally did. His mind had already turned to Olivia and the growing distance between them, for which none of them seemed prepared or capable of bridging. Overcoming his burdened feelings, he worked on his story throughout the day. But now, even the writing that had served as his escape seemed tense.

He felt as though every word he typed was pulling him farther into the knowledge that his relationship with Olivia was falling apart and that there was nothing he could do to stop it. Ethan realized he couldn't continue to ignore the issue by the time the sun went down. He needed to face the growing quiet between him and Olivia by having a conversation with her. However, he was afraid that doing so might permanently shatter them. He walked to Olivia's studio that evening, his heart racing as he got closer to the well-known structure. He could see her silhouette through the glass, hunched over her canvas, totally engrossed in her work, the lights on inside.

Ethan hesitated a moment. He was aware that everything may alter the moment he stepped through that door. However, he couldn't continue to act as though everything was fine when it wasn't. He inhaled deeply before pushing the door open and entering. The air smelled of paint and turpentine, and Olivia looked up as she walked in, her face expressionless. She wiped her hands with a rag and said, "Hey." "You weren't what I expected." Ethan shut the door after giving a nod. "I had to come see you." Olivia looked at him for a while, scrutinizing his face. "Is everything all right?" Ethan started to reply, but the words became stuck in his throat.

He was unable to communicate to her how he felt or how the quiet between them was choking him. Rather, he approached her with cautious, patient steps. His voice was full of emotion as he murmured softly, "Olivia, we need to talk." Olivia's expression softened, and she put down the rag with understanding and sadness in her eyes. "I understand," she muttered. "I've also been experiencing it." For a considerable amount of time, they stood silent, the tension between them evident. Ethan desired to touch her, to embrace her, to somehow close the gap that had developed between them. However, he knew that this would not suffice. Not now.

Ethan's voice was hardly audible above a whisper as he eventually uttered, "I don't know what to do." "I have no idea how to resolve this." Olivia's fingers twisted together as she stared down. "Neither do I." Ethan recognized that this was the moment he had been dreading as the silence dragged on, oppressive and thick. This was the critical juncture where everything they'd built and shared was in jeopardy. For the first time, he questioned their ability to reunite. With a trembling voice, Olivia whispered gently, "I don't want to lose you." "How can I meet your needs, though?"

Her words made Ethan's heart hurt, and he forced himself to swallow in order to control the surge of feelings that threatened to overtake him. He muttered, "I also don't want to lose you." "However,

I can't continue to act as though this is sufficient." Olivia hurriedly pushed away the tears that welled up in her eyes. "I understand." Ethan understood then that their mutual silence had communicated more effectively than any words could.

Chapter Eleven-The Collapse

When Ethan woke up, his phone was vibrating steadily on the nightstand. He reached over and grabbed the device while groggily rubbing his eyes. His heart didn't stop because of the time or the messages, but rather because of how bright the screen was in the early morning light. That one was Olivia's. They were straightforward—just a few words—but they struck him in the stomach. I'm leaving town for a little. When I return, I will give you a call. Blinking, Ethan sat up in bed and read the note again. Still dazed from sleep, his mind found it difficult to comprehend what he was witnessing. Are you leaving town? For a time? About this, he had heard nothing.

They had not even discussed her leaving. Only a few days prior, they had finally faced the growing stillness between them and had the last meaningful conversation. However, she had avoided mentioning her departure. With his mind racing, Ethan threw the phone back on the bed and got up to pace his bedroom's cramped quarters. What kept her from telling him? Where was she heading? What was she doing?

OFF THE BEATEN HEART

The knot in his chest tightened the more he considered it. This was no ordinary journey.

At the very least, Olivia had a purpose for her sudden disappearance. The sting of her comments grew worse as Ethan mentally relived their most recent exchange. I'm uncertain about how to fulfill your requirements. That sentence has haunted him ever since, echoing through his mind. Ethan had thought they might find a way ahead, even if the meeting had ended in uncertainty. They stood in her studio, facing the truth they had been evading for weeks. They were able to resolve their differences. Olivia, however, was on her way. She hadn't even told him, either.

Ethan reached for his phone without thinking and dialed her number. It rang once, twice, and three times, then went straight to voicemail, and his heart thumped. He paced once more, cursing beneath his breath as he felt frustrated. What was she doing? In his hand, his phone buzzed. Olivia had texted me. Ethan, I need some time. I'll elaborate later. Time. Space. When things became too heavy, she would consistently ask for the same things. She had utilized these identical items to keep them separate. However, this—this seemed unique. It was like being abandoned.

Ethan put on some clothing, got his keys, and left the house with the intention of facing Olivia before she vanished. He couldn't let her go in this manner. He couldn't leave without conversing, or at least comprehending her thoughts. He rolled down the window, relishing the cold morning air as he drove through the quiet streets towards her apartment, the sun still low in the sky. As he arrived at Olivia's building and saw her car already loaded with bags, his chest constricted. Now she was going. A knot of terror and rage tightened in his stomach.

This seemed like an escape, not just a matter of time and location. A retreat. He parked and got out of his car, walking quickly and urgently to the front door. Everything he had been holding within since their last talk—everything he wanted to say to her—was racing through his head. He required clarification. He had to understand why she had withheld this information from him.

The sound reverberated in the still early air as Ethan banged on the door more forcefully than he had planned. It was a moment before Olivia eventually emerged, her expression a mix of astonishment and fear at his presence. "Ethan," she murmured in a quiet but wary tone. "Why are you in this place?" He tried to maintain his composure as he added, "I could ask you the same thing." "You're simply heading out? Without informing me?

With a sigh, Olivia walked out onto the porch and shut the door. She appeared to have not slept much, as evidenced by her rumpled clothes and twisted back hair in a loose bun. She said, "I was going to tell you." "I just had to sort it out first.""Figure out what?" Ethan inquired, growing irritated. "You didn't even mention that you were considering going," Ethan said, his irritation growing. I learned about it through a text message. Olivia, what's going on?

Olivia folded her arms across her chest and declared, "I'm heading to an art retreat." "Ethan, I need time. It's time to reflect. to mentally organize my thoughts. As her words took hold, Ethan gazed at her, his heart lowering. "Time to consider what?" Olivia averted her gaze, her jaw clenched. "About us. Almost anything. The earth seemed to be slipping away from Ethan. "So you're simply going to go? without first speaking with me? Without allowing me the opportunity to— Olivia cut in, "I'm not fleeing, Ethan," in a stern but sympathetic manner. "All I need is room." I can't do that here; I have to work things out on my own.

Ethan shook his head, hurt and rage clenched in his chest. "That's not possible here? Why not? Why can't you just have a simple conversation with me? Olivia, we can work this out together. With sorrow in her eyes, Olivia muttered, "I don't know if we can." "I'm not sure if we can fix this." Ethan stepped back, gasping for breath as her words hit him like a kick to the stomach. He knew their relationship was under stress and in danger, but he never imagined it would reach this point."Are you uncertain about our fixability?" His voice trembled with emotion as he repeated. "What exactly does that mean? Are you simply going to walk away without making an effort?

Olivia combed through her hair, her countenance troubled. "Ethan, I'm not implying that I don't care about you. However, I've been feeling disoriented, unsure of how to be with you at the moment. Before I can even consider us, I must rediscover who I am. Every time she spoke, Ethan's heart ached, and he gulped hard. "So what? Are you simply going to vanish for an indeterminate amount of time and expect me to wait for you to resolve the situation?" Olivia murmured quietly, her eyes sparkling with unshed tears, "I'm not asking you to wait." "All I need is time." Ethan shook his head and repeated, "Time," with a sour tone. "Isn't that what you need constantly?" Space and time. But Olivia, what about me? How about what I require?" Olivia's voice was little more than a whisper as she gazed down. "I apologize."

Both of them remained silent for a minute as the apology lingered between them. As Ethan attempted to make sense of what was occurring, his heart was thumping and his mind was racing. Although he knew that their relationship was shaky and that things were tough, he hadn't anticipated this. He didn't think she would simply leave. "Are you certain you won't be coming back?" Finally, Ethan spoke in a hollow voice.Olivia's eyes welled up with tears, but she took a while to respond. Instead, she reached out and gently touched his arm. Her voice trembled as she answered, "I don't know." "I have no idea what will occur. However, I must do this. As the truth of what she had spoken set in, Ethan gazed at her with a broken heart.

She wasn't simply going on a getaway out of town. She might be leaving him behind for good. Ethan said in a heartfelt tone, "I thought we could figure this out together." "I believed that we had something genuine." Olivia nodded and blinked, a tear running down her cheek. "We did," she murmured. However, I need to assess my readiness for what you're seeking. I can't accomplish that while I'm here. The weight of her words was crushing down on Ethan more forcefully than he could handle, making his chest feel as though it was collapsing.

Despite his secret knowledge that he could do little to stop her if she had already left, he was determined to defend her and demonstrate to her that they could overcome this. He stepped back and stared at her, breathing heavily. "Well, is this it?" Olivia shook her head, her eyes watering, and took a moment to react. "I'm not sure," she muttered. "I simply must leave." As she turned away and went back inside, Ethan stood there, watching her with a broken heart. He knew it wouldn't matter if he followed her and pleaded with her to stay. He couldn't reverse Olivia's decision, she had already made it. His mind was racing with the knowledge that he had been deceiving himself all along, and his chest felt hollow as he made his way back to his car. He had never been able to get what he needed from Olivia. And she was gone now.

Chapter Twelve- Self Reflection

Following Olivia's departure, the first several days passed quickly. Ethan walked past them in a stupor, proceeding with his daily activities, yet feeling as though a part of him had vanished. Her abrupt departure echoed in his thoughts like a half-remembered dream, terribly present yet bizarre and far away. She was no longer there, and her absence was more noticeable than ever. He found reminders of her everywhere he looked: the paintings she had leaned against the wall, the notebook she had scrawled in, and the cup of tea she used to leave half-finished on his counter.

The most painful aspect was the stillness. There were no more spontaneous studio visits or phone calls. Once a place of mutual creativity, the silence between them now seemed to go on forever.

Ethan initially attempted to occupy the quiet with work. Though the words didn't come as effortlessly as they used to, he immersed himself in his writing and was determined to keep going. He couldn't help but think of Olivia whenever he sat down at his desk—her laugh, her smile, the way she always seemed so far away, even when she was sitting right next to him. Nevertheless, he pushed through the emotional haze to write, but the result was unfiltered, jumbled, and unsure.

He had no idea how to interpret it all. A part of him felt upset, even indignant, that she had departed before they had a genuine opportunity to resolve their differences. A quieter, more reflective side of him, however, questioned whether he had been requesting something she would never provide.

Ethan had to face some difficult realities in the isolation that followed Olivia's departure. He had always yearned for something tangible and enduring. Like so many things in life, he had yearned for the stability of a relationship that was based on permanence and wouldn't fade. Olivia, however, had never been that way. The need for permanence had never constrained her, and she had always lived in the present moment. She had told him that from the start, but he had refused to listen.

One night, while he was sitting by himself at his desk and looking at his laptop's blinking cursor, Ethan wondered if he had been attempting to shape her into someone she was not—someone she would never be. He had tried to control Olivia, to keep her inside the parameters of his own desire for stability, even though he had fallen in love with her unpredictable nature, wildness, and capacity to make him feel alive. And in doing so, he had disregarded the core of her identity.

As the realization weighed heavily on him, Ethan sat back in his chair and ran a hand through his hair. Was he mistaken all along? Was his conception of love too inflexible, too preoccupied with permanence and control? He had always believed that love required construction, developed gradually, and gained strength through dedication. However, love had always been about moments rather than forever with Olivia. It was impossible to record or preserve the beautiful, fleeting moments.

He reflected on their discussions and the evenings they had spent discussing the meaning of love, and he now saw that Olivia had been correct in her own way. Without attempting to fit love into a schedule or a box, she had lived completely in the now and embraced it for what it was. In contrast, Ethan had consistently been preparing for an uncertain future. Perhaps that had been his error.

Ethan struggled with these ideas for weeks, thinking back on his connection with Olivia and its significance to him. He tried to unravel the complex web of emotions that had accumulated inside of him by taking long walks through the city and allowing his thoughts to roam. He questioned whether he had been overly preoccupied with his desires and his search for something enduring when Olivia had provided him with something worthwhile—something that was impervious to time and permanence.

As he gave it more attention, he realized that love—at least in Olivia's interpretation—wasn't about dominance. Building walls to keep things safe and secure wasn't the goal. It was about realizing that some things should be experienced rather than clung to.

Ethan opened his laptop and started writing one evening when he was sitting by the window, watching the rain fall against the glass in steady streams. However, the words arrived in a different way this time. He was no longer writing to steer the story. He wasn't looking for solutions or answers. Rather, he allowed his words to come forth organically, capturing the tumultuousness of his feelings, the ambiguity of love, and the beauty in life's transient nature.

His book began to shift from being about a character trying to cling to something tangible. The protagonist's quest shifted from seeking assurance to accepting the unknown. Ethan felt as though he was writing honestly for the first time in weeks, even though it was untidy, unpolished, and intensely personal. He was just letting the reality of his interactions with Olivia dictate the plot; he wasn't attempting to write a flawless tale.

As he was writing, Ethan realized that love might not fit into any category or description. It had nothing to do with predictability or permanence. It was about accepting the other person for who they were, not for what you wanted them to be, and about being in the moment. That occasionally required letting go.

Ethan missed the beauty of their relationship because he had wanted Olivia to be someone she wasn't. Even if their relationship didn't turn out the way he had hoped, it had been genuine. The times they spent together—the late-night talks, the creative energy they exchanged, the depth of their bond—were genuine and significant. They had been significant, even if they weren't permanent.

Ethan reclined in his chair and gazed at the words on the screen, experiencing an odd calmness. Although he still felt the pain of Olivia's absence and missed her, he now realized that clinging to her would have required him to ask her to be someone she wasn't. And that was control, not love.

Ethan kept writing in the ensuing weeks, using his book as a means of processing what he had discovered about love, himself, and the intricacies of interpersonal interactions. Even though he had no idea whether he would ever see Olivia again or if their paths would cross again, he had come to terms with the fact that their time together had been worthwhile.

As the book came to a close, Ethan understood that the narrative he was narrating had nothing to do with locating the ideal companion or relationship. It was about letting go of the need to control the outcome, finding beauty in the fleeting moments, and learning to accept life's impermanence.

In that insight, Ethan found a sense of liberation he had not known he was seeking.

He understood that love wasn't about forever. It meant living in the moment, enjoying it, and letting go when the time was right.

Ethan grinned to himself as he typed his novel's last sentence, feeling lighter than he had in weeks. For the first time in a long time, he felt OK with the fact that he didn't know everything and that he didn't know where life would lead him.

Sometimes, the beauty of love doesn't lie in clinging to someone.

Learning to let go was the key.

Chapter Thirteen - Reconnection

Ethan was just finishing up his laptop after a long day of writing when he received the text in the late afternoon. It was brief and somewhat cryptic, resembling something Olivia would write before she was ready to give the sentences her whole attention. *This evening, stop by the studio. I'd like to speak. Ethan gazed at the message, feeling a wave of emotions wash over him, his heart racing. Weeks had passed since Olivia's departure—weeks of solitude, introspection, and the loneliness that only someone like her could endure.

He had attempted to come to terms with her absence—to acknowledge that perhaps their time together had ended and that their bond had never been intended to endure. She was reaching out now, though. And everything altered as a result. Ethan paused, pondering what to say for a second while his thumb lingered over the screen. There was a part of him that wanted to ask why she had gone, what she had been thinking, and why she hadn't spoken out before she vanished. The responses didn't bother him because he still wanted her.

All he needed was to see her, hear her voice, and understand what remained between them. He typed out an answer at last: I'll be there.*

Shadows lined the streets on the customary trek to Olivia's studio as the sun sank below the horizon. The world seemed silent, almost anticipatory, as though it was also anticipating what would happen next. Ethan attempted to suppress the questions, uncertainties, and hopes that were racing through his head. He had convinced himself that he had found peace in their separation and that he was fine with letting go.

However, as he got closer to her studio door, all of those meticulously built barriers started to come apart. He stopped at the door, inhaled deeply, and then knocked. There was silence for a while as the boom reverberated softly in the calm evening air. The door then cracked open, revealing Olivia standing there with the warm light leaking out from within, framing her silhouette. She spoke gently, "Ethan," with a hint of hesitancy and something else in her voice, something deeper that he couldn't quite identify. "Olivia," he answered, sounding more composed than he actually was. The smell of paint and turpentine filled his nostrils as he entered.

Although there were new paintings strewn throughout the walls—bright, colorful pieces that felt distinct from the work she had previously done—the studio was just as he remembered it. She shut the door after him, and they stood there for a while, the silence between them thick with silenced words. Her shoulders were a little more bent, as though she were carrying a burden she hadn't been able to release, and Ethan observed the small shifts in her expression as he examined her. She had the same appearance but also a completely distinct one. Olivia broke the silence with, "I'm glad you came." She pointed to the couch in the room's corner. "Want to take a seat?"

Ethan followed her to the couch and nodded. There was a noticeable tension between them as they sat down, a range of feelings that neither of them seemed prepared to confront directly. They remained silent for a while, the burden of their common past bearing down on them. Olivia finally added, "I've been thinking about us," in a hushed voice that was unexpectedly vulnerable for Ethan. "Almost everything that took place." Ethan, his heart pounding in his chest, made a small movement. "I must have." With her hands firmly gripped in her lap, she looked down and nodded. "Ethan, I left because I didn't care about you."

I left because I was unsure of how to meet your needs. I couldn't decide which way to go and felt as though I was being dragged in two different directions, suffocating. As she spoke, the old, familiar ache in Ethan's throat deepened. "I never wanted to make you feel like that." "I simply didn't know how to give up what I desired." I believed we could figure it out if I hung on strong enough. Olivia gazed up at him with a mix of love and sorrow in her eyes. "I understand. I've been struggling with that issue. I adore your concern and your intense attachment to things. I'm not like that, though. I don't know how to stay rooted in one place or one person the way you expect me to.

When Ethan realized that they had been postponing this talk for so long, he gulped hard and felt his heart ache. His voice was filled with emotion as he continued, "But that's what I've been trying to understand." " Perhaps I have been requesting something that isn't available. Perhaps permanence isn't what love is all about. Consider enjoying each moment rather than trying to prolong it.Olivia reached out and put her palm over his as her gaze grew softer. Her voice trembled a little as she replied, "I've been thinking about that too." "I've been considering us, including you. And I realized that perhaps I've been avoiding my emotions and the thought of showing vulnerability to someone. Maybe I was just afraid, but I told myself I didn't want to feel restrained.

As her words took hold, Ethan's chest constricted as he gazed at her. "What are you afraid of?" She whispered, "I am afraid of losing myself." "Of being harmed. I've witnessed the results of people's attempts to make something last. When things collapse, they end up broken. I didn't want to experience that. However, I believe I wounded you in the process of defending myself. As he listened to her, the unvarnished honesty in her voice broke through the barriers he had erected over the last few weeks, and Ethan's heart broke.

He had always known Olivia was terrified of commitment, but hearing her acknowledge them and seeing the anguish in her eyes made him realize how profound her worries were. Ethan said, "I was scared too," in a voice that was almost audible above a whisper. "Afraid to lose you." I'm afraid you'll leave me if I don't hang on tight enough. With tears in her eyes, Olivia shook her head. However, Ethan, you didn't have to cling on so firmly. I simply wanted some room to sort things out, and I wasn't leaving. I also didn't want to lose you.

The weight of their confessions hung between them as they sat in silence for a long time. As they at last started to face the reality of their relationship, Ethan experienced a mix of relief and heartbreak as the tension between them both decreased and increased. What does that leave us with, then? Ethan inquired in a low voice, his tone doubtful. Olivia wiped a tear from her cheek while maintaining eye contact with him. She was honest when she said, "I don't know." It's unclear if I can give you the stability you need.

I don't want to lose you, though. I don't want to leave what we have behind. A mixture of fear and optimism filled Ethan's emotions. Hearing her express that she didn't want to lose him made him miss her even more than he had already. However, he was also aware that nothing had altered in a significant way. He was still the one who required more than moments, and Olivia was still the free spirit she had always been. His voice was full of emotion as he said, "I care about you, Olivia." "I can't express how much I care for you. However, I'm uncertain whether I can continue to live here, as I'm never sure where we stand.

With a wounded gaze, Olivia nodded. "I understand. Furthermore, I don't want to continue to cause you pain by failing to provide you with the information you require. Despite their intense love for each other, they struggled to reconcile their basic differences as they sat there. Yes, they were in love, but their relationship was complicated, full of expectations and worries neither could handle. Olivia whispered quietly and tremblingly, "I don't have the answers." However, I am certain that I want you in my life. Ethan, I don't want to lose you. Her words made Ethan's heart tighten.

The idea of leaving her now, after everything, felt unthinkable, as he had missed her more than he could articulate. But concurrently, he realized that they couldn't keep traveling in the same direction, hoping for different outcomes while repeating the same behaviors. "I also don't want to lose you," Ethan said in a broken whisper. "However, if we're constantly worried about what might happen next, I'm not sure if love can endure like this." Olivia extended her hand and slipped it into his, her fingers tightly twisting around him.

She said, "Perhaps love isn't about knowing what's coming next." "Perhaps it's simply about being present at this moment and letting the rest work itself out." Ethan gazed at her, a mixture of love and doubt weighing heavily on his heart. He had never understood how to love without considering the future, nor had he ever known how to live in the present. However, observing Olivia's vulnerability in her eyes, he pondered whether she might be correct. Perhaps love didn't have to be about stability or permanence. Perhaps it was about accepting each moment rather than trying to control it. Ethan felt a peculiar calmness descend upon him for the first time in weeks. He lacked all. He was uncertain about his and Olivia's future, and he was searching for answers. However, that might have been acceptable. Perhaps the definition of love didn't require assurance. Perhaps it simply had to be felt.

Ethan came to the realization that perhaps—just perhaps—love was sufficient as they sat together in the silence of her studio, their hands clasped together. even though it wasn't permanent. For now, it was sufficient. And that was all he required for the first time.

Chapter Fourteen - The Final Verse

Ethan's desk lamp's gentle glow illuminated the scattered pages of his book while casting long shadows throughout his apartment. With the cursor blinking after the last phrase, he gazed at the screen before him. It was finished. After months of writing, editing, and giving every word his all, he finally finished his novel. Nevertheless, he felt anything but relief as he sat there and gazed at the lines he had just penned.

A knot of emotions entangled between doubt and satisfaction made his chest feel heavy. His account, which drew from the depths of his turbulent relationship with Olivia, was heartbreakingly personal, intimate, and honest. Every syllable and chapter conveyed the intricacy of their relationship—its beauty, its ambiguity, and its unavoidable impermanence. He felt exposed in a way he hadn't anticipated because it was the most honest thing he had ever written.

Leaning back in his chair and stroking his hair, Ethan shut down his laptop. He looked around the room at the crumpled bits of paper he had tossed aside in irritation, the notes all over the place, and the empty coffee glasses. While reading this book, he processed everything that had happened between him and Olivia. Now that it was over, he had no idea what would happen next.

He reflected on Olivia and the evening they had spent together again in her studio. He could still clearly remember her sitting across from him with her hand in his. They hadn't promised anything about the future, and they hadn't settled anything that evening. However, they had a genuine bond that defied easy categorizations like "together" or "apart." It was messy and complex, but it was them. And that was sufficient for now.

A part of him couldn't get rid of the persistent feeling that he was deluding himself, despite his steadfast belief that love didn't have to be permanent in order to be significant. Was this recognition of impermanence a revelation or merely a way to get out of the laborious task of creating anything enduring?

He was distracted from his thoughts when his phone buzzed on the desk. Kate, his agent, had sent him a note requesting an update on the book. For weeks, she had been excitedly awaiting it, checking in from time to time and gently reminding herself to send it over as soon as it was ready. Ethan couldn't help but feel guilty for not joining in on her excitement because he knew she was excited—likely more so than he was.

He took a deep breath, reached for his phone, and texted her back, saying,I've completed it. Tomorrow, I'll send it your way.

He put down the phone and got up to go to the window. A multitude of lights flickered in the darkness as the metropolis loomed before him. He stood there thinking for a long time, wondering whether the novel's completion had helped him better understand himself or if it had merely made him more confused.

In many respects, the book had come to reflect his relationship with Olivia. A writer like Ethan, the main character, had fallen in love with someone who symbolized everything he wanted but could never have. Their love was passionate but fragile, always on the verge of breaking. The protagonist of the narrative grappled with the same issues that Ethan had encountered in real life: Could love endure in the absence of permanence? Was accepting the transient nature of connection narrative grappled and living in the moment sufficient? Or was that merely a pretext to avoid making a commitment or facing the vulnerability that accompanies creating something genuine?

Ethan had given the character's journey his whole attention while writing it, examining all facets of love, fear, and doubt. Now that the story was over, he wasn't sure if he had come any closer to discovering the answers. The reader's interpretation determined the protagonist's fate, just like his own.

Was love like that? A never-ending list of queries with no definitive answers?

Returning to his desk, Ethan opened the laptop once more and browsed the last few pages of the manuscript. There was a sense of bittersweet acceptance in the final chapter, which marked the end of the protagonist's quest. There was an underlying sense of mistrust that persisted despite the character's learning to let go and accept the transience of love. Though he acknowledged that love didn't have to endure forever to be significant, he couldn't help but question whether he had overlooked something more profound and enduring in his quest for independence.

Ethan contemplated revising the novel's last lines while he gazed at them and kept his fingers hovering over the keyboard. However, this was not the narrative he had intended to tell. Like love itself, it was not flawless. Perhaps that was the purpose.

Ethan forwarded the manuscript to Kate the following day. Kate responded almost instantly, sending him an enthusiastic, ecstatic email that expressed her pride in him and her eagerness to begin work on the tale. As he read her words, Ethan grinned, but the same feeling of conflict persisted. He was aware that this was excellent work, possibly his best, but it felt lacking in some way. The story itself didn't feel lacking, but rather the emotions it stirred within him.

Kate called him a few days later, her voice brimming with excitement. Without making an effort to be polite, she continued, "Ethan, this is it." "This is the one. It's unvarnished, exposed, and I'm at a loss for words. This is your best work to date.

As Ethan sat on the couch, she continued to talk about how readers will undoubtedly find resonance in the concepts of love and impermanence as well as the protagonist's journey's emotional depth. However, he experienced an odd feeling of disinterest as she talked, as though he were hearing someone else's tale.

When Kate finally stopped to catch her breath, he replied, "Thank you, Kate." "I'm happy you find it satisfactory."

"All right? "It's fantastic," she emphasized. "Ethan, this is going to be a big deal. People will see a completely different side of you.

Even though it didn't meet his expectations, Ethan smiled. "I hope so."

Ethan sat silently after they hung up, gazing at the manuscript on his laptop. He knew he should be thrilled because this was the culmination of months of hard work and the pinnacle of everything he had endured. However, instead of feeling a sense of satisfaction, he was overcome with a crippling sense of uncertainty.

He had used the book to analyze all of the emotions he had experienced with Olivia, including the highs, lows, love, and fear. Now that it was over, he wasn't sure if he had found any clarity at all. He was still struggling with the same doubts that he had during the writing process. Was love really about embracing impermanence? Or was that a means of evading the more difficult and messier task of commitment?

Ethan got up and went back to the window to gaze at the city below. He reflected on Olivia and their previous discussion in her studio. They had always kept things vague and open. Neither he nor she had promised anything. However, their relationship remained unbroken and unresolved.

Was that sufficient?

The main character in his book had come to accept that love didn't have to endure forever to be significant. However, Ethan pondered whether he had been too hasty to embrace that same notion for himself as he stood there, gazing out at the world outside his window. Was he letting go because it was the right thing to do, or because it was simpler than having to confront the fact that true, lasting love might need more than he had been prepared to provide?

The solution remained a mystery to him, as it had through the novel's composition. He felt more torn than ever, whereas he had hoped that by the time he got to the last chapter, he would have found some sort of closure.

Perhaps that was how love worked. Perhaps it was meant to be unclear, disorganized, and confounding. Maybe the experience was the only way to fully understand it, and a story couldn't neatly encapsulate it.

Ethan realized that he didn't have to know everything as he stood by the window and watched the sun set behind the metropolitan skyline. He didn't need to understand whether love was fleeting or eternal. He needed to experience it, felt it profoundly, and that it had molded him in ways he was still unable to fully comprehend.

Perhaps that was sufficient.

Ethan took a long breath before returning to his desk, opening his laptop, and typing the last words of his book.

Love is not a material possession. It is a part of your existence.

He pressed save, shut down the laptop, and relaxed as a sensation of silent acceptance descended upon him. For the time being, it was OK that he didn't know everything.

Sometimes, the quest for solutions wasn't the essence of what made love so captivating.

Learning to live with the questions was the key.

Chapter Fifteen - The Choice

The late afternoon sun hung low in the sky, bathing the river in a golden glow. There was a light wind blowing through the trees along the bank, and the air was warm. In that place, Ethan and Olivia first discussed love, the future, and commitment, clinging, and letting go. Even though a lot had changed since that day, Ethan still felt the weight and importance of it all the more as he waited for Olivia to come.

He recalled how certain they had been of their opposing opinions, like two people on opposite sides of a huge chasm, when they had first spoken by the river. Olivia had talked about how love was a fluid concept that defied categorization or assurance. Ethan, on the other hand, had always thought that love required construction to endure. However, Ethan was no longer certain of his views after everything they had experienced, all the nights he had spent doubting them, finishing his work, and exposing his own doubts.

The crunching sound of footfall on the gravel walk startled him out of his revelation. He turned to see Olivia approaching him, her body glowing softly in the last rays of the light. She appeared both familiar and far away, as though he had known her for ages but was seeing her for the first time. Ethan hadn't previously noticed—or maybe hadn't let himself see—the peaceful strength and calmness in her expression. She came gently toward him with a cloth-wrapped object. Her movements were purposeful, as though she was aware that this exchange—this moment—would alter everything. They remained silent for a while as she approached him, with the sound of the river flowing gently in the background.

Olivia's voice was firm but compassionate as she continued, "You came."

Ethan gave a nod. "I was unsure if I would."

Olivia looked into his eyes with a small smile. "I didn't think you would want to."

They were silent for a long time. It seemed like their relationship was still stressed from all they hadn't said in two weeks.

Olivia finally broke the stillness. She handed out the cloth-wrapped bundle and carefully opened it to reveal a painting, one of her masterpieces. "I brought something for you."

Ethan stared at it, breathing heavily. On the canvas, a tumultuous, swirling pattern of bold reds, deep blues, and vivid yellows appeared to clash and meld simultaneously. Olivia had never painted anything like it before; it was vibrant and dynamic, as though the colors themselves were living. It was stunning, yet untamed and wild. similar to her.

Olivia stated softly and with emotion in her voice, "This is me.""This is who I am, my life, and my heart. It doesn't follow any rules, it's unpredictable, and it doesn't fit into tidy little boxes. But it's brimming with love and passion. I want you to know what it means to love me, which is why I'm giving you this.

As he took the painting from her, Ethan's hands shook a little, and he traced the unpredictable, vivid color strokes with his gaze. The gravity of what she was delivering and the weight of her words weighed heavily on him.

Olivia inhaled deeply while maintaining a steady stare. "Ethan, I need to understand whether you're capable of loving me in this manner." You should not expect me to change who I am. without requiring definitions or assurances. Just accept me for who I am, despite the confusion and uncertainty that accompany it.

Ethan's thoughts were racing when he gazed at the painting, his pulse thumping in his chest. She had always hoped that he would embrace the wild, untamed nature of love and let go of his need for certainties. After spending so much time clinging to something solid and enduring, the idea of love not needing control confronted him. It might resemble the hues on this canvas—meaningful in their transience, lovely in their disarray.

Mixed feelings constricted his chest as he glanced up at Olivia. A part of him wanted to say yes, to embrace the fact that nothing was certain and fall headfirst into this erratic love with her. Because it seemed overwhelming and uncontrollable to fall headfirst, his intense love for her worried him. However, a part of him still yearned for the security he had always desired, for the kind of love that remained strong throughout time and grew stronger with each passing day.

Olivia murmured gently, her voice shaking a little, "I don't want to lose you." But rather than loving me as you wish me to be, I need you to love me for who I am. I need to know if you are capable of loving me as I am.

Ethan felt the weight of her words fall on him like a blanket as he swallowed hard. He turned his gaze away from her and toward the river, where he saw the water flowing steadily past, constantly shifting and moving. similar to life. Similar to love.

He reflected on all they had experienced together, including their disagreements, intimate times, growing quiet, and the frankness of their most recent exchange. He reflected on his book, the lessons he had discovered while writing it, and the protagonist's development of an acceptance of love's transience. Now, he stood at a crucial juncture, faced with the need to make the same choice.

Would he be able to let go of his demand for consistency? Could he come to terms with the fact that love, like the river, was constantly flowing and changing, and perhaps that was sufficient?

Olivia watched him from a distance, fear and hope shining in her eyes. She was waiting for him to decide about the type of love he believed in, as well as about their relationship.

His hands felt the weight of the painting, the tumultuous swirl of colors matching his inner turmoil. A part of him wanted to embrace the chaos and the unknown and have faith that it would be sufficient to dive right into the crazy love she was providing. However, a deeper, quieter part of him continued to believe that love required stability and roots to flourish.

Even when everything around it altered, the river continued to flow by steadily and unwaveringly.

With his heart pounding in his chest, he turned his gaze to Olivia. Her gaze swept over his face as she waited for a response. She had given him everything she had—her life, her emotions. Whether he could love her for who she was without expectations or conditions was now up to him.

Ethan started to say something, but the words stuck in his throat. He glanced at Olivia, then back at the water, then down at the painting he was holding.

He understood then that the decision was about more than just love.

Everything was at stake. He was contemplating life, his ideal way of living, and whether he could embrace the unpredictability that had always filled him with fear.

As he prepared to respond, he inhaled deeply, his heart pounding.

However, the story came to an abrupt halt before he could finish speaking.

The river continued to flow.

Olivia waited as well.

Concluding Thoughts

Really, what is love? Is it the fleeting, strong spark that burns hot and then fades, or is it the constant, unchanging connection that endures over the years? These were the same questions that had plagued Ethan since he first met Olivia, and he was still struggling with them as he looked at the final page of his book. Like their relationship, the novel was a mirror of the inconsistencies and complexities of human connection, reflecting this ambiguity. Long thought, love had to be permanent to be meaningful, Ethan thought. In his view, true love was something you created and endured through life's ups and downs. Literature and films praised his parents' solid, dependable, and enduring love.

Olivia, however, had challenged all his preconceived notions about love. Instead of promising him eternity, she had given him moments—bright, lovely, and short. That was the origin of the tension. Throughout the entire book and, in many ways, his entire relationship with Olivia, Ethan found himself torn between these two concepts. On the one hand, stability offered security and comfort; it was the kind of love that didn't require you to jeopardize everything. However, there was also the thrilling anarchy of uncertainty, the wildness of living completely in the moment without caring about the future.

Olivia taught him that love could be messy and uncontrollable without losing its authenticity. Olivia had embodied that wildness. Despite Ethan's acceptance of that notion, a part of him always yearned for more. In order to make their love last, he wanted to keep her. There, the key question arose: Could love endure without the guarantee of permanence, or was that just a ruse to avoid the vulnerability of true commitment? The book ultimately left that question open-ended, just as it did with Ethan and Olivia's relationship. After all, life rarely provides the solutions we are looking for, particularly when it comes to emotional issues.

Instead, the grey zones, the liminal spaces between certainty and uncertainty, where love can be both liberating and limiting, beautiful and painful, often remain for us to negotiate. Ethan had to experience this firsthand. He had occasionally lost sight of the true meaning of love—an encounter, a moment, a bond that didn't require definition or control—in his quest for permanence.

Even though Olivia didn't match the model he had always imagined, he had discovered something genuine. Their love was chaotic, but it was intense, profound, and beautiful. However, despite his acceptance of their love's transience, Ethan couldn't get rid of the issue that kept coming back to him: Was pleasure possible by accepting impermanence, or was it a means to avoid the difficult task of creating something lasting? Was he letting go out of moral obligation or because it was simpler than confronting the anxieties associated with commitment? Since there were no simple answers, the narrative didn't address these questions. In actuality, love was neither one thing nor the other; it wasn't necessarily ephemeral nor eternal. It could be either depending on the people, situation, and time of day.

For Ethan, the journey had been about accepting that not all love stories had happy endings and learning to live with that uncertainty. While some love was destined to burn bright and then fade, leaving behind lessons and experiences that would last a lifetime, others were designed to last only a short time. Perhaps that was sufficient. Stories that offer us a sense of closure, resolve unresolved issues, and culminate in a satisfying conclusion often captivate us as readers. However, things are rarely that straightforward in life. Ethan's narrative serves as a reminder that love is contradictory, just like life. It can simultaneously be both short-lived and long-lived, chaotic and stable, painful and happy.

Even though love doesn't last forever, it has the power to shape, challenge, and develop us—perhaps this is what makes it so beautiful.Ethan ultimately made no decision regarding his future with Olivia. He was not required to. The choice was to learn to live in the liminal space between both extremes, to understand that love could exist without assurances, rather than to choose between permanence and impermanence, stability and chaos. Ethan realized that his love was beyond definition and control as he stood by the river with Olivia's artwork.

It wasn't about holding on too tightly or trying to squeeze someone into your preconceived notions. Being present, accepting the messiness and unpredictability, and letting your emotions run deep—even at the risk of heartbreak—were all parts of love. And that's where love's real power resides. Its power is not in its durability but in its capacity to transform us and open our eyes to fresh perspectives on the world and ourselves. If Ethan and Olivia had experienced something genuine and significant, even briefly, it was more important than whether they could maintain their romance.

What is love, then? Is it the wild, erratic spark that comes and goes, or is it the consistent bond that lasts over time? Perhaps the answer lies in the fact that love encompasses all of these aspects. It is what we allow it to be and what we make of it. The knowledge that we don't have to choose between the two is sometimes the best gift that love can offer us. We just have to leave things alone.

STRAIGHT FROM THE HEART

Thank you so much for taking the time out to read **"Off the Beaten Heart."** I hope Ethan and Olivia's journey resonated with you as deeply as it did with me during my writing. I would greatly appreciate an honest review of the book on this or another book review platform you frequent. Your feedback not only helps other readers discover the book but encourages me too as an author. If you're curious about what the future holds for Ethan and Olivia, I would love to hear your thoughts. Should their story continue? I'm excited to explore where their paths might lead next, and your input could help shape their future.

Thank you again!

Rowan Pierce

Milton Keynes UK
Ingram Content Group UK Ltd.
UKHW031145311024
450535UK00001B/5